BABALA'S CORRECTION

By
Bethany Amber

Published worldwide in 2014 by

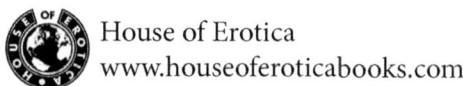 House of Erotica
www.houseoferoticabooks.com

An imprint of Andrews UK Limited
The Hat Factory
Bute Street
Luton, LU1 2EY

Copyright © 2014 Bethany Amber

The rights of Bethany Amber have been asserted in accordance with sections 77 and 78 of the Copyrights, Designs and Patents Act 1988.

All rights reserved. No part of this publication may be reproduced, stored in a retrieval system, or transmitted in any form or by any means, without the prior permission in writing of the publisher, nor be otherwise circulated in any form of binding or cover other than that in which it is published and without a similar condition including this condition being imposed on the subsequent publisher.

All characters appearing in this work are fictitious. Any resemblance to real persons, living or dead, is purely coincidental.

Contents

Chapter 1	1
Chapter 2	21
Chapter 3	36
Chapter 4	60
Chapter 5	70
Chapter 6	83
Chapter 7	96
Chapter 8	117
Chapter 9	132
Chapter 10	135
Chapter 11	153
Chapter 12	175
Chapter 13	179

BABALA'S CORRECTION

Chapter 1

Babala was naked and the forest was cold. Rain dripped through the thick canopy of leaves, making the girl's body slick and silky in the arms of her captor.

Unheeding of her captive's chill the Lady Fazath jogged with a long, easy, loping stride along the narrow winding path. She cradled Babala in her strong arms as easily as if the girl was a wraith and no heavier than a sack of feathers, rather than shapely flesh, delicately formed.

The night was dark and seemed endless, and Babala rested her head upon the moulded bronze that served as her mistress's breastplate. It was hard against her pale cheek, which felt bruised by the rhythmic bouncing through the forest. The only comfort was the warm grip of her ladyship's hands. One held Babala firmly about her naked thighs, just below the gentle swell of her buttocks, and the other cupped a bare breast. Her ladyship tweaked it, making the pink nipple painfully tight. This brought a blush to Babala's cheeks, for it was not as if she yearned the touch of a woman. Her sexual experience was very limited and restricted to one man - not a lover, but a man who was employed by the Prince to prepare the girls of the harem for his use.

Babala shuddered in her captor's arms as she felt the memory, like a physical thing, of the Taskmaster's cock, thick and hard, slipping easily through her maidenhead after hours of sensual preparation. It began by him making her stand with legs wide apart before a looking glass. Had not Babala been the narcissistic maiden that she was her skin would have burned with blushes at this lewd instruction - and at what followed.

'Peel back your love lips, my sweet,' he commanded. 'And tell me how you feel.'

Babala remembered slight flushes stain her cheeks and she bowed her head as she did as she was ordered. Gently, with her forefingers, she opened her outer love lips just a fraction.

'Wider,' he snapped, and she felt the sting of an open palm upon the fullness of her bottom cheeks. 'And don't pretend shame.' The palm slapped her again. 'Thrust out your love mound and look into the glass with your head held high. Girls like you are self-absorbed,' he added knowingly. 'You like to see your pretty little clitties peeping from their hoods, all pink and shiny. Admit it!' The palm slapped again and Babala could feel the heat as well as the sting. 'It's true, isn't it?'

She lifted her head and, obediently, looked straight into the looking glass. Humiliated though she was, she opened her love lips to the full and saw her sex bud, shining and erect in her virginal slit.

'You are so delicious, Babala,' he said, tapping the open sex with the very tip of a finger. 'So unusual, as well as so pliant and obedient; so different from the usual maidens I have to suffer here.'

He taunted her playfully with fingers and tongue for many minutes, teasing her bud until a less disciplined girl would have screamed.

As he finally took her completely she was overcome with ecstasy when his cockstem was pulled from her fully and then pushed back, grating her erect clitty as it re-entered. She remembered arching her body over the damask couch upon which he had laid her, and thrusting her pussy mound hard against the crisp curls of the Taskmaster's groin, the better to feel her approaching orgasm.

'Yes, my darling one,' grunted the Taskmaster. 'You clutch my cock and pet its length most expertly. For an inexperienced maiden you are a proficient lover. It will always be so, believe me. I know a willing girl when I feel her cunny gripping about my cock.'

Babala thought she would faint with the pleasure of her come. She wanted more, but the Taskmaster had already passed her on to the women who would bathe her, cleanse her cunny of his issue and dress her in the short silk shift the Prince required his girls to wear so that their freshly opened cunts were freely available to him.

She shuddered afresh. The memory did not fade, but rather became more painfully clear in her memory and a terrible feeling of loss stole over her. If only she could escape, but the Lady Fazath was so strong and powerful, so full of vigour. Even with her rain-slicked body, slippery as silk, the girl had no possible chance to escape from this Amazon of a woman.

True, dressed in a light armour of a snugly fitted breastplate and a short white skirt, the Lady Fazath was dressed for speed rather than battle, although battle she would surely do if the occasion arose. Her muscular arms, the skin a gleaming tawny gold, were bare apart from the broad silver bangles tight about her smooth biceps. A beaten silver belt cinched her waist with a dagger tucked neatly into it, and the short skirt swirled about her taut buttocks that rippled with power as she ran.

Lustrous midnight hair flowed about her broad shoulders; the shining curls dancing in the double moonlight of Ellipsis. Her onyx eyes slanted as she skipped lithely over fallen logs and her fine patrician nose sniffed the air for any sign of danger. The handsome lips had the softness of a girl's, but were wide and firm as a man's.

Babala, slender as a willow, fragile as the finest porcelain, but fetchingly voluptuous, was destined to be the Prince's favourite had not the Lady Fazath intervened. She scarcely succeeded in stifling a sob and was squeezed unmercifully by the muscular arms that held her.

'Stop that!' The words were hissed in her ear and the outpouring of breath stirred the damp cascade of her golden curls. 'Did you really want to be the Prince's plaything until he tired of you and tossed you aside like so much kitchen refuse?'

'It was my destiny.' Babala's soft voice was all but inaudible above the steady patter of the rain and the rhythmic pounding of the Lady Fazath's feet. They were more a thought than spoken word. She knew the Prince was especially taken with her stunning beauty, her ripe breasts and splendidly shapely hips and legs. Hadn't he told her so in just those words? He picked her out from all the girls freshly trained by the Taskmaster, who told her, at his final and intimate inspection, that she could be the Prince's consort if she behaved herself.

Unable to contain the quiver of misery that made Babala slip in her captor's arms, she almost slid to the leafy and muddy ground. A muscular limb gripped her like a vice and a hand as hard and smooth as a paddle was laid sharply upon her vulnerable buttocks. She felt the hot sting of the chastisement and felt her bottom flesh shudder under the blow.

'You are mine, girl.'

'I was to be the Prince's,' Babala retorted boldly.

Smacks far harder than the first single slap fell one after the other upon Babala's rain-wet and glowing bottom.

'You dare to question my actions, you little strumpet? Me? Second only to the Taskmaster in importance at the castle?' The queries were growled thickly from deep in the womanly breast.

'He wanted me! The Taskmaster told me. And you will never be able to return to the castle now. Never! We are fugitives.' The girl wept in earnest, her tears blending with the rain that glossed her finely formed features. Amazed at her own boldness, she continued. 'You had no right to steal me from the Castle Ellipsis, and you are a woman. What possible use could I be to you?'

Laughter, full-throated and deep, rang through the forest, and the Lady Fazath gently set Babala on the wet ground. The girl's limbs fell naturally into a sensuous pose, the slender arms were swept up above the golden head, the full breasts pouted firmly and were pert, the shapely legs parted, but twisted to reveal the glowing bottom, tinged from the severe slaps that had been so recently delivered to the pale skin.

'What use?' Cool fingers stroked the heated hillocks of her bottom, and suddenly Babala was hauled to her feet and pressed against an oak tree. Her wrists were held above her head by the Lady Fazath's strong fingers. Her smacked bottom chafed against the rough bark and her breasts were further chilled by contact with the mistress's bronze breastplate. The girl felt the sensitive flesh of her nipples spring to hard and painful erection once more.

'What use?' Lady Fazath whispered again, changing her grip upon Babala's wrists to hold them with one hand while the other slid over shapely ribs and upwards to the firm lower slope of a breast.

The stroke made Babala shudder, not this time with misery cold or fear, but with a strange kind of excitement, not unlike that she remembered feeling in the arms of the Taskmaster. But surely this could not be? The Taskmaster was a man and the Lady Fazath was a woman.

Lips, as cool and smooth as the silk spun by the silkworms in the mulberry trees in the castle grounds, closed upon the bud of Babala's tautened nipple. Her smarting bottom, pressed so hard against the bark, arched towards the woman's lower body. The puff of golden curls upon her mound brushed against the white silk Lady Fazath wore about her narrow hips and this, too, sent a further quiver of naughty excitement through Babala's helpless body.

'You think you are so knowing,' said the Lady Fazath, her words muffled by the fulsome flesh of Babala's breasts. Teeth grated gently on one wrinkled nub, biting and yet not biting upon the tautened skin and sending a wicked frisson of longing to the inner hub of the girl's body; that delicious parting of flesh lips hiding the newly opened haven. 'Oh yes, you girls, all opened by the Taskmaster's flesh sword, think you are so knowing and worldly, but you know nothing of the beauty of a woman's love. In that way, my sweet, you are still a maiden.'

Babala gasped as strong fingers slapped her thighs apart, smacking the tender flesh until she was forced to open her legs - but strangely, liquid far warmer and creamier than rain seeped to gloss the golden fronds of her sex nest. She gasped again as fingers that were firm, but sensually gentle, spread her nether lips.

'Now this,' whispered the Lady Fazath, finding Babala's nubbin, 'tells me that you are greatly aroused by my touch.'

'No,' denied Babala, but she knew this was not true. She felt her nubbin hard and probing out of its little hood. It throbbed against the Lady Fazath's touch and drew back and forth between her fingers. It was wet and slippery with the cream that seeped from the very depths of Babala's body.

'Deny all you like,' murmured the Lady Fazath, sinking to her knees on the leaf-strewn forest floor, uncaring that her bare legs became smeared with mud and leaves.

Body arched in unbidden passion, Babala thrust against the busy fingers and heard the mistress chuckle, but the sound was soon muffled as lips and tongue replaced fingers in the creamy private place. The soft lips sucked upon the hardened nubbin and Babala threw back her golden head in ecstasy. Rain dripped through the oak leaves and splashed into the upturned sapphire eyes that gazed sightlessly through the forest canopy. She could feel her nubbin throbbing on the Lady Fazath's expert tongue, and a glorious feeling grew inside her just as it had done when the Taskmaster opened her maiden passage.

'Oh, please...' Babala murmured. 'Oh please, no. You must not... I must not. Oh, please, no more!'

Lady Fazath immediately stopped the caresses and Babala felt the chill of loss. Her nubbin throbbed uselessly, cream glossing its inflamed tip.

'Do you really want me to stop?' murmured the Lady Fazath, gripping Babala's spread thighs with vice-like fingers.

Unable to help herself, Babala bore her hips down. 'No,' she admitted meekly, 'I don't want you to stop.'

'Do you want to finish your come, my pretty?' urged the mistress.

Babala remained silent, only swaying her nether regions about the Lady Fazath's upturned and handsome face, and blows of such force were rained upon the girl's tensed thighs that she mewed with pain, and yet the slaps only enhanced the liquid warmth she felt between her cunny lips.

'Answer me!'

'I - I want to come,' Babala admitted between her sobs.

'And do you want me to make you come?'

Remembering the time the Taskmaster made her delirious with happiness as he speared his cock through her maidenhead, Babala remained silent.

'Admit that a woman's love is more gratifying than a man's,' ordered the Lady Fazath. 'Otherwise I shall not kiss your nubbin again.'

'Oh, no...' Babala bore her bottom down upon her ladyship's upturned face and felt a new sensation. There was a warm moistness, a gentle pressure at her secret hole, the tight one that the Taskmaster did not enter. A tongue, she thought, blushing furiously, and it was licking her bottom hole. Horrified at such intimacy she gasped and drew herself upward, but she was pulled down again.

'Admit it.' The order was a rough growl, animal-like in its fervour and muffled by Babala's open sex flesh.

'I admit it,' Babala sobbed gratefully, as lips closed once more about her nubbin.

From somewhere deep in the forest, but still faraway, drifted the faint sound of running feet, but the woman and the girl were too engrossed in taking mutual pleasure to take much heed. Babala could feel the steady throb of her approaching climax, the build up of pleasure within her depths, drawing up from her cunny to her breasts.

Lady Fazath drank the girl's creamy issue, which was pleasingly copious, and felt the fluttering of flesh on her busy tongue. She would teach this young hussy how to give pleasure to a woman, she vowed, pushing her fingers between her rain-soaked thighs to rub her own aching clitty...

'The girl is one of those made ready by the Taskmaster.' The speaker was heavyset, muscular, but his stride was light and easy over the muddy ground. In one hand he held fine thongs of leather that he stroked over the bulge at his groin, barely covered by a roughly fashioned leather skirt. 'They are trained to please a man.'

'But this one, Graf,' said one of his three companions, 'is different.' Young and wiry, tense in his stride, he stayed close to the older Graf. He was dressed in a short leather tunic like the others, but there was no masculine bulge between his thighs. He was nervous of their assignment to return the two women to the castle.

'You whinge like a girl, Peli,' said another. 'Have you thought what fun we can have when we catch them?'

'Bart's right, and what I look forward to is to truss the Lady Fazath with her legs spread and her arms stretched high above her head, naked as the day she was born.'

'From what I've heard, Capel,' said Peli, his voice low with nervousness, 'she will not let a man near her, let alone make her helpless.'

Capel, a giant of a man, larger even than Graf, roared with laughter. 'We are four. I doubt she'll best us.'

'She is a trained warrior,' argued Peli. 'Don't be so sure.'

'I'll strip the bitch and splay her on the ground,' grunted Capel. 'I'll take each tit in my mouth until she begs me to fuck her. I'll tease her. Spread her cunt lips and use the handle of my flail to open her up a little, my hearties. For as you know, my cock is the terror of all the women in Ellipsis.'

The other men, apart from Peli, chuckled in agreement.

'And what of you, Peli?' asked Graf. 'What do you desire of these females?'

Peli would have stumbled had not Graf caught his arm. 'In truth,' he mumbled, his chin low on his chest, 'I wish we were at home in the castle guardroom. I've heard that the other one, Babala, is a magical creature who can turn a man to stone should he pole her with his cock.'

Again the others laughed.

'Aye,' said Bart, 'if you say so. But I hear tell that her nubbin is as prominent as a little cock, straining from its hood, anxious to be petted and excited to a come which will leave her begging to be fucked by each of us, one after the other.'

'No one knows this for sure,' said Peli.

"T'is true!' Bart insisted. 'As true as I stand here. The Taskmaster's manservant told me and the Taskmaster himself told him.'

'But the women belong to the Prince,' groaned Peli, 'just as we do.'

The four men ran along the narrow path in silence for many minutes, each keeping his own council until Graf spoke at last, never slowing his pace. 'Well, I shall keep quiet about our pleasure in the forest, if I can trust you all to do the same.'

'For the sake of spearing her silken cunt,' said Bart, 'I would be willing to have my tongue cut out by the root.'

'And to torment the Lady Fazath until she begs for more I should be willing to be made a eunuch,' Capel said gleefully. 'What say you, Peli?'

'Leave the lad alone,' snapped Graf. 'He has tasted no woman yet.'

Capel slapped his thigh triumphantly. 'Just as I thought! The lad's a virgin, his cock undipped and an orgasm not known except by his own hand.' He chuckled cruelly and prodded Peli's back as the lad hung his head in shame and blushed with confusion and embarrassment.

At that very moment Graf held a warning finger to his lips, ordering silence. 'Listen!' he hissed.

The men stopped and obediently strained their eyes in the darkness, watchful of the path ahead. They craned their necks and cocked their ears. Capel, especially, cupped a hand to his ear and turned his head to focus on any unusual sound in the forest.

'I hear nothing but rain,' he said irritably. 'I say we should press on and find the bitches before they escape beyond the borders of Ellipsis.'

'No, Graf's right,' said Peli, 'I hear something. A sound... a soft sound... as if...' He looked at Graf, searching for help in describing what he could hear.

'That's the sound of pleasure, my boy,' supplied Graf. 'The sound of an orgasm, welcomed and enjoyed.'

'They are near,' whispered Bart. 'Just up ahead, and the Lady Fazath is using the maid for her own ends.'

'Circle,' whispered Graf, pointing the directions in which the men should go. 'But tread like ghosts through the forest. Surprise them as they take their pleasure.'

Peli was the first to come upon them and he gasped at the sight that greeted him. The Lady Fazath was on her knees between the shapely spread legs of Babala, who had her head flung back in uncaring bliss. His eyes darted down once more to the woman on her knees. He saw a flicking tongue and the bud that it teased. The others were right; it was truly beautiful, thickened and throbbing, slick with spittle. He felt his organ swell beneath the soft leather of his tunic and his fingers circled his thickness, sliding up and down as he watched the two females.

'There you are, lad.' It was Graf who whispered and crept up beside him. 'This won't do. Pleasuring yourself when you should be binding them.' He tugged at the silken cord at Peli's waist. 'What are you thinking of?'

'Babala's cunt,' Peli said hoarsely. 'It is beautiful, isn't it? I wish I could kneel between her legs instead of her ladyship. I want to taste her, to suck her, to make her groan like madam did just now.'

'All in good time, my lad,' Graf said with a low chuckle, freed the silken cord at his own waist, fashioned from it a long loop, and with an easy throw he tossed it expertly over the two writhing figures. It spun silently through the air and tightened about them, holding fast. A shriek rent the forest, followed by a howl of rage as they were dragged, together, through the mud and rotting fallen leaves. Babala began to sob and cupped her hands about her cunny, trying to hide the soft flesh from the sight of the men.

'I'll have you hanged for this!' screamed the Lady Fazath.

'We're only following orders,' said Bart, who had appeared in the clearing and was looking hungrily at madam's muddied skirt and the silken midnight thatch bared beneath it. 'You seem a little moist and flushed between your thighs, mistress, if I may say so.'

'You may not say so!' With a hiss of rage the Lady Fazath, with something of a struggle in view of the bindings about her and Babala, drew her knife and threw it in Bart's direction. Deftly he dodged and the knife fell harmlessly into the undergrowth.

'And now it's my turn,' he grunted, and slipped his hands between the two roped females and bound the mistress's wrists with another length of cord. With the Lady Fazath rendered almost harmless the men were free to busy themselves on the girl.

Peli, on Graf's orders, bound Babala until he had her body arched, her wrists tied to her ankles, but her knees kept fully apart by a stout length of branch. 'Do you wish to fulfil your desire, my lad, before we take them somewhere less cold and wet?'

Babala's eyes, wide and deep blue as the most rare of sapphires, were moist with tears, making them luminous in the rain-soaked half-light. She looked at Peli, her soft lips trembling and her cheeks still flushed from the orgasm so recently experienced. Her breasts quivered, the teats taut and inviting, and Peli felt his cock rise more stiffly under his tunic, thrusting at the fine leather to poke, full and proud, like a tent pole.

'Go on, lad,' urged Graf, pushing the young man forward. 'Or shall I sling her about my neck to make her more available, so you can tongue and prod with your fingers to your heart's desire.'

Babala strained at her bonds and felt the silken cord grow tighter at her wrists and ankles, to cut more painfully into her flesh.

'Don't you dare touch her!' The Lady Fazath writhed slowly towards Babala across the muddy ground, her progress impeded by her bonds. 'She is mine! Do you understand? Mine!'

A whip cut the damp air with a fearsome crack and Capel stood over her ladyship, a triumphant grin on his coarse face as the woman grunted in pain and the muddied skirt was cut by the lash across the slight swell of her belly, fully baring her lushly bushed sex mound.

'We were given to understand she was the Prince's, mistress,' he said scathingly. 'Which is why we were sent after you.'

The Lady Fazath rolled onto her belly to hide her partial nakedness. 'The girl had her fill of the coarseness of man when she was fucked by the Taskmaster.' Her words were full of venom and she tried to crawl towards the girl she so desired, surprised when she flinched away from her touch.

Babala gasped. 'Not true,' she whispered. 'The Taskmaster's cock is beautiful, skilful. He did not hurt - '

'Be quiet, stupid girl!' Lady Fazath again tried to writhe sinuously over the slimy ground, trying to reach Babala, to protect her.

'Yes, be quiet,' echoed Capel, and the long whip cracked through the air once more to land, this time, upon the Lady Fazath's upturned buttocks. The blow was so heavily laid that the ill-treated silk skirt fell in shreds about the woman's tawny hips, leaving the taut hillocks of her bottom bare for all to see, and a glowing red welt crossing the mounds from the upper hip to the lower swell of her buttocks. Capel sank down upon his knees and lifted his tunic, thrusting his groin toward the Lady Fazath's face in a lewd fashion.

'Hateful creature,' grunted her ladyship. 'Filthy man.'

But for all her protestations Babala could not help noticing that the Lady Fazath's eyes were riveted, for many moments, upon the dark bloated shaft which speared up from Capel's crisply curled groin. Babala frowned, trying to interpret the strange expression. Could her ladyship's tastes be not all that they seemed?

But then madam again lowered her eyes, diverting them from Capel's hugeness. 'You are a man,' she rasped. 'I have naught to do with men.'

'So I hear,' Capel goaded, smoothing a huge hand over madam's pouting buttocks, paying particular attention to the scarlet welt which stood proud across the paler mounds. 'Which makes it all the more interesting for me, your ladyship.' He let a thick finger trail lightly in the crevice between the taut buttocks and grinned when he felt the quiver of flesh under his touch.

Babala closed her eyes, not wishing to see the Lady Fazath humiliated further, knowing as she did how she protested against their coarseness. Then a scream began low in her throat as she felt herself lifted high in the air and the sensation of hair against her back. Fearfully, she allowed her lashes to flutter open, and was slung above the ground about the thick neck of the man called Graf. Although she could not see exactly how open and vulnerable her cunny was, she could feel the bough pressing into the tender skin of the inner side of her knees, spreading her open, and her body flushed at the humiliation of being laid so bare in front of these strangers.

'I can see the flesh glistening and droplets coating her open gully,' said a timid young man's voice. It was the lad, Peli.

The man who held Babala about his neck chuckled. 'The gully is her opening, my lad. Some call it a quim, others call it a cunt. The droplets are to ease the entrance of a good stiff cock.'

Babala tried to squirm in her humiliation, but Graf held her still, making a sign with his fingers that Peli should touch her sex. Turning her head painfully she saw the sign and it made her blush more deeply. This was so different from the only other time a man used her body - the Taskmaster. He was so gentle, making sure she was ready, massaging balm about her cunny that made her nubbin spring to stiff and swollen erection. She remembered how pleased the Taskmaster was at this, how he complimented her and told her that the Prince would delight in her.

'Come along, lad,' Graf's voice interrupted her thoughts. 'The rest of us are waiting to take our turn. Touch her. Dip your fingers into her wetness. Touch her clitty until you bring her to a satisfying come.' He chuckled and held Babala round his neck with one hand, while the other circled his stiffened cock. 'I doubt you will be able to contain your spunk once you do that.'

'Why don't we go to the caves and get out of this rain?' said Bart testily. 'They're not far from here, and we can use the females at our leisure. Then we can be on our way back to the castle.'

'A good idea,' said Graf, already starting down the path. 'You can feel her to your heart's content there, lad.'

Babala could see Peli's disappointed face as he followed the older man down the path.

'You'll hang for this!' shrieked the Lady Fazath. Naked, she was slung about Capel's neck, her wrists and ankles bound like Babala's.

'And you will not?' said Capel, a chuckle breaking his voice.

Bart led the way, eager to reach the caves, and Babala could feel the first rays of the sun, warm and dry upon her. As they entered the wide opening of the first cave Graf, with a sigh of relief, lowered Babala to the soft sand that formed the floor. He knelt beside her aching body and gently eased the branch from between her knees, then taking his knife from his belt he cut the cord and allowed her limbs to ease free. Unwittingly, she fell into a sensuous pose, her arms above her head on the sand, her breasts uplifted with the teats hard and taut while her legs spread invitingly.

'She asks for it,' growled Bart, and he lifted his tunic to hold his cock stiffly forward, his sturdy thighs parted. 'Is it true she has only recently lost her maidenhead? She acts like a whore, to my way of thinking.'

'She's trained!' hissed the Lady Fazath. 'Trained to be sensuous in all ways. Don't you dare demean her by calling her a whore!'

Babala screamed as the Lady Fazath felt the sting of Capel's whip, so he turned on her and pointed a warning finger. 'Do you want the same, bitch?' he growled.

'We're wasting time,' said Bart impatiently.

'That's right,' Capel agreed. 'Let's get on with it and then return to the castle. Who will be first, my lads?'

'None of you,' rasped her ladyship, throwing herself headlong upon Babala. The sound of naked skin slapping against skin was loud in the cave. Peli gave a nervous laugh and Bart cleared his throat.

'Now, now,' he chided. 'It's our bit of fun, you see. As guards we get little chance to relieve ourselves with the harem girls. Allow us that - just this once.'

'Never!' hissed the Lady Fazath.

'Then take the consequences.' Capel's face was a mask of fury.

Babala whimpered as she felt madam hauled roughly from her and saw her thrown to the sandy floor by the huge man. She heard her ladyship scream as Capel's cock probed at a cunt that had known no man's before.

'Don't hurt her,' Babala begged.

'And what of you?' asked Bart, standing over the girl, looking between her inviting legs. 'Can we hurt you?'

Babala's eyes strayed to Peli as if in supplication, but he held back, watching as Bart stroked a stout thumb across the outer margins of her cunny lips, smoothing the fair curls away from the slit, opening it until Babala could not help but part her legs yet further and arch her mound in a gesture of offer.

'Is this what you were taught at the castle?' he rasped. His mouth was close to her cunny curls now and she could feel the heat of his breath. Nodding meekly she tried to close her eyes, but an open palm slapped her pale cheek, rocking her head from side to side and making her eyes snap open in shock. 'Look upon my cock, girl,' he ordered. 'Is it not as fine as the Taskmaster's? As stiff, with the skin as smooth and the globe as silky?'

As if far away Babala could hear the Lady Fazath moaning softly and she turned her head to look into the gloom at the back of the cave. She could see two men, Graf and Peli, eagerly rubbing their cocks, which throbbed and pulsed as she watched. They aimed the warm and creamy issue that spilled from them upon Lady Fazath's open mouth, and some spillage splashed into the flowing cascade of midnight hair. Capel was pumping into her cunny with his gnarled thickness and she could see his taut balls slapping her ladyship's buttocks as she lifted her legs higher and tighter about his waist. He had surely changed madam's preferences, thought Babala, with an unbidden and secret smile.

'Answer me, girl,' ordered Bart. 'Is not my cock as fine?'

'Indeed it is, sir,' answered Babala, coming to her senses. 'It is so fine that I should dearly love to caress it with my lips and tongue.'

'And will you take young Peli into that mysterious cunny of yours at the same time?' asked Bart, his voice husky with lust. 'And perhaps Graf into your bottom hole lying beneath you?'

'If that is what would please you, sir,' Babala said meekly, remembering all the little nuances taut to her by the Taskmaster.

'Oh, it would please me just fine,' grunted Bart as he polished the shining globe of his cock with the tip of his forefinger. Babala could see its tiny opening, appearing and disappearing as the finger slipped back and forth. A globule of pre-issue oozed from the pore and spilled warmly upon her forehead. 'It is decided then,' Bart croaked eagerly, beckoning to Graf and Peli.

Through the gloom Babala could see the Lady Fazath thrown upon her belly, her buttocks raised to feel the kiss of Capel's whip. The woman was not moaning, but mewing, a sound that could be either pleasure or pain. Capel's eyes were bright with lust as he flung the whip over his shoulder to expertly flick the lower reaches of madam's buttocks and merely kiss her cunny lips with the very tip. The touch was no more than a tickle, a tease that could only serve to heighten her ladyship's desire.

'You, Peli, kneel between her thighs and fuck her.' As Bart spoke he was spreading the outer leaves of Babala's cunny, once more to reveal the dark and gleaming flesh.

Peli, rubbing his cock to full stiffness, eager to feel the thrill of orgasm over and over again, threw himself to his knees. He looked so young, so handsome, so innocent, like the pages at the castle, and yet she had heard Graf say he was a fully trained guard. His body trembled, but Babala could not discern whether this was apprehension or passion.

Holding out her arms she invited him to lie between her spread thighs, but immediately she received a finger slap upon her breasts, first one and then the other, bringing her teats to hard and painful erection and making her breasts swell, pout and glow.

'Allow Graf to slide beneath you, strumpet,' ordered Bart. 'Allow him to pole your bottom entrance or it will be the worse for you.' He cast a telling glance at Fazath, who was now whimpering loudly as each lash petted her bottom.

'But, sir,' pleaded Babala, 'my bottom hole is still virgin and very tight. Have you not some balm or salve to ease its opening by?' Her stomach knotted with apprehension as she looked at Graf's thick length.

'Kneel,' the latter ordered, 'I shall ease it with spittle and my tongue. Guards do not carry such luxury easements.'

'And while you're about it, spread your legs,' commanded Bart, as Babala crouched low on the chill sandy floor of the cave. The grit grated on her knees and shins and, as she crouched lower, it rasped against the fine flesh of her breasts, so recently slapped. 'Let young Peli finger your cunt; the lad is aching to feel its wet warmth.'

Babala did as she was bid and spread her thighs wide. She could feel Graf tugging at the plump flesh of her bottom cheeks, pulling the cleft open to reveal the taut bud of her rose-hole. Quivering, she felt Peli's fingers tentatively spread the puffy leaves of her cunt, stroke the hardened bud of her nubbin and finally plunge two fingers into the darkness of her creamy depths. She was in a quandary. They had called her a whore because of her pliancy and willingness, and yet she was only doing as she was trained to do. Should she struggle? Should she close her legs and fight for her modesty and chastity?

A wetness filled the pit of her rose-hole and she knew that Graf had filled his mouth with spittle and aimed the slimy globule at her secret entrance. Peli's fingers slid in and out of her cunny and she found herself bearing back, despite her fears, upon the pleasant sensation, felt her clitty throbbing with a growing fullness.

'Open your mouth,' rasped Bart. 'Wide.' Babala raised her head and saw him kneeling before her, his cock stiff and smooth in its fullness. 'And I do not wish to feel those sharp little teeth, biting and nipping. Open very wide.' He waved the smooth globe of his cock across her lips and Babala could taste the salty bitterness that she knew was the taste of a man's spume.

As she slowly began to engulf the thick throbbing length she felt a pressure at her bottom hole. It was not unpleasant, especially with the added sensation of Peli thrusting his fingers in and out of her sex and thumbing the very tip of her nubbin. The pressure grew as Graf eased his tongue-tip into the wrinkled pit of her rose-hole. She bore back against it, encouraging the intrusion.

At the back of her tongue she could feel the smoothness of Bart's globe and taste the first driblets of his come. The Taskmaster had taught her the taste, a pleasant bitterness that was a compliment to a woman's skill with her lips and tongue. She almost gagged as Bart thrust deep into her mouth to the very entrance of her throat, but she relaxed her muscles and the thickness slipped back and forth easily.

Graf's tongue was fully inserted in her bottom hole and was dipping in and out, but Babala felt no shame at this secret opening being breached, only pride that she had learned yet another technique to please a man. Soon, she knew, she would have the honour of taking Graf's cock into this secret opening.

Had her mouth not been so full of Bart's pulsing length Babala would have gasped at the next pleasure she was afforded. Another tongue, Peli's, entered her cunny, slipping in and out and sucking at her copious juices. Though she tried she could not take more of this, and much as she attempted to hold back her climax, she could not.

And it came, in great body shaking waves. It seemed it would never stop, that she would die from pleasure. It left her limbs weak and trembling. She spread her legs to their fullest extent and felt her sex clutch upon Peli's tongue and her bottom hole suck upon the three fingers Graf had gradually inserted into its tightness, and without fully realising it she drank down the copious gush of Bart's spunk, swallowing its creamy warmth.

'She is ready,' grunted Bart, as he pulled his thickness from her mouth. 'Throw her over upon her back, Peli.'

They spread her, her arms and her legs to their fullest extent, tying her wrists with cords and pegging them to the sandy floor with their daggers. It was not as if she had the will to run, she thought, as Graf positioned himself beneath her, prodding her prepared bottom hole with his newly stiffened cock. That done Peli trembled above her, taking quick stabs at her still throbbing cunny with his own shaft before finally sinking into its silky depths. Again Bart thrust his own flesh sword between her lips and welcomed the caress of her tongue.

Babala was glad she had been relieved of the problem of choice. Bound to the floor she had no option than to lie there and allow the men to have their way, to do whatever they wished to her. And if she thought the straining efforts of the three men caused an orgasm to end all others, she was not wrong. They took her to the verge of madness with their pleasuring and her body welcomed their energetic release.

Chapter 2

The roguish guards took the two women over and over again. Babala felt an ache in her bottom and a soreness in her cunny caused by the pumping in and out of erect penises.

During their imprisonment in the caves the two were used again and again. In frustration, the men took up their flails or whips and lashed the women if their cocks did not rise to full stiffness, so Babala was marked with dark welts upon her bottom, the slight swell of her tummy and the fullness of her breasts. The Lady Fazath, too, bore the marks of whips upon her tawny skin and, although she had fought like a tigress, she was no match for the four trained guards.

At last the men fell into an exhausted sleep and Babala, too, was allowed to rest. The Lady Fazath crawled across the floor of the cave and took the girl in her arms, cradling her golden head upon her full breasts.

'There, my sweet,' cooed her ladyship, 'sleep now and remember what I told you of the coarseness of men. After this I doubt you will ever wish a man to touch you again.' The woman cupped the sore and heated pouch of Babala's cunny, holding it softly and smoothing away the drools of male come with her own gentle fingers.

But they were not all coarse, thought Babala. Peli was especially gentle with her, and he had turned his eyes away when Graf and the others lashed her; the brutes delighting in the sight of her pale skin being marked with flails and whips.

As she sank into a troubled sleep, her lovely face nuzzled between the Lady Fazath's breasts, she remembered her excitement as she waited, only days ago, to be prepared by the

Taskmaster. There was a tingle of excitement in her belly, the flesh rippling at the very sight of the master's manhood.

She'd waited in a queue of girls outside the preparation room. Some wept and some were taken to the punishment box, over which they were thrown to be whipped into submission. Some, who were especially naughty, were taken into the castle grounds and put between the shafts of small pony carts. Babala had watched all of this and saw how the girls were lashed to the shafts with leather thonging and driven naked along gravel paths until abrasions marked their feet and the lashes wielded by the punishment guards reddened their backs and bottoms.

She watched as they were brought back to the preparation room and serving woman soothed their wounds with salve. They were dressed once more in fine lawn shifts, sheer as gossamer, which all the girls wore as they waited their turn.

Babala looked at them with pity, saw the trembling breasts and the dark shadows of their pussy mounds clearly, prettily fluffed up with special combs by the serving women. If a girl's bush was too full it was trimmed and the upper thighs were shaved to smoothness no matter how much they protested. If they still continued to weep and hold back when they were called to take their turn with the Taskmaster they were thrown into the dungeons and chained to the damp and mossy walls until they came to their senses.

When at last it was her turn, Babala entered the anteroom and bowed her head as she had been taught. She placed her hands upon her golden waves of hair to show that she was entirely submissive and willing, and only then did she lift her head to look into the dark eyes of the man who would take her maidenhead.

He complimented her upon her willingness to please. 'Good girl,' said the Taskmaster. 'Excellent.'

She stood passively as he stroked the fullness of her breasts through the fine material of the gown. With her hands upon her head these were lifted prettily, inviting his caresses. Unlike the naughty girls she was looking forward to his taking of her innocence, and her destined life in the Prince's harem.

Boldly, with her sapphire eyes invitingly wide, she smiled at him. He was a huge man and towered above her, naked apart from a square of jewelled leather tied about his narrow waist with a thong. The skimpy garment scarcely covered the upright thickness of his cock. He slipped the leather to the side, giving her sight of it. Even with her excitement heightened the way it was Babala had to gasp at its length and girth, at the almost spherical globe that was bare of foreskin and gleaming with his pre-issue.

'Are you ready for this, my girl?' he asked in his deep tones.

It was then that he did the test with the looking glass, making Babala lift her gown and part her legs, thrusting out her mound and spreading her sex lips. When she carried out his orders obediently he was pleased and knelt before her, giving her little kisses upon her open cunny.

Babala's legs shook with anticipated pleasure and she could feel her cunny pulsing with pre-orgasmic shudders.

At last he rose to his feet. 'What a pleasure to have such a yielding girl; it has been a difficult morning and I fail to understand why these girls present themselves to be part of the Prince's harem if they must be punished to make them amenable.'

Once more he petted her breasts, feeling their heaviness and the smooth lower slopes. He fingered each teat through the gossamer, pulling them to tautness. 'These are beautiful,' he said, his voice full of genuine admiration. 'The very sort in which the Prince delights.' He ripped open the fine cloth, making Babala blush at this sudden exposure, and placed his lips about each. Then he draped the sheer material over each and began to suck the pink teats through it, until the wet cloth clung to her nipples, showing the qualities that would please the Prince to perfection. The touch of his lips was incredibly sensual and Babala thought she might swoon with pleasure if he continued.

'Time to relieve you of the gown, my girl,' he said at last, lifting his head and smiling into her eyes. He walked away from her and took a pair of scissors from an instrument table, and Babala could not help wondering: why bother with scissors when he had ripped the gown open to her waist?

After a moment's hesitation he took up something else, items that glowed in the flickering light of the many candles set about the room.

Trembling as the gown was cut from ankle to throat and fell away to lie about her feet in a soft puddle of white, Babala ventured a look at the table from which the Taskmaster had taken the scissors. It was covered with many instruments; manacles, dainty whips, porcelain pots of salves and balms, as well as lengths of chain, the sight of which made her shudder, not from fear, but with breathless apprehension.

Naked before him, her hands again obediently clasped and linked upon her head, Babala could feel the brush of his cock upon the skin of her lower belly. She felt a quiver of longing ripple through her fleshpot and hoped he would not notice it and think her forward.

'These may pinch a little, my dear,' he said, and Babala lowered her eyes and saw silver clips in each of his large hands. There were tiny teeth on each prong of the clips and she shivered as she imagined the pain. He opened them and stroked the sharp teeth against the base of each puckered bud of her nipple. She shuddered again, but it was not from fear, she was sure. Very slowly, the Taskmaster closed the clips over each bud, and Babala gasped.

'The pain is quite exquisite, is it not, my love?' he whispered huskily. 'Delicious... you cannot believe how those tiny pains will enhance the beauty of my entrance into your body.'

A scarcely audible mew came from Babala's full lips as the clips tightened upon each teat. She felt her breast flesh swell, the skin of her lower belly flutter and a moistening of her fleshpot.

'You look more beautiful than ever, my sweet,' said the Taskmaster, admiringly. His hands rested for a moment on the curve of Babala's hips, feeling the gentle shelf of them. 'And now it is time for me to examine your potential.'

He led her from the anteroom to another inner chamber. It was darker than the first, with fewer candles placed about. Exotic scents filled the air that made Babala's head spin and her legs scarcely able to support her.

A shadow in the furthest corner of the room shaped itself into a chair as Babala approached it. Her arms ached from being held so long upon her head. Her breasts became more swollen and her teats sore with every step, and yet it did not feel like torture. It was a much more delicious sensation.

As they reached the chair, the clear sight of it made Babala's belly become liquid with excited apprehension. The back of the chair sloped steeply away, and at each corner of the tilted seat were stirrups upon which dangled wide leather straps.

'To spread your legs nice and wide,' he explained unnecessarily, and her imagination ran riot over what she would feel once strapped in the chair. She already felt a coolness in her fleshpot as if it was already fully open, and strange draughts of cool air wafted over the heated lips and inner leaves.

He lifted her into the chair. Babala felt the chill of the leather seat upon her bottom and felt her buttocks spread open. The Taskmaster's eyes twinkled as if he knew exactly the sensations she was experiencing. An involuntary quiver ran through the whole of her body as he placed one ankle into a stirrup and tightened the broad leather strap, and then her feeling of helplessness increased as the second ankle was placed in position and strapped in place.

'A pleasing sight, my dear,' he said, his eyes never leaving her nest. 'And you please me by leaving your hands so meekly upon your head. The Prince likes his girls to be naturally passive and vulnerable.' He trailed a finger about the swollen perimeter of each breast, nodding with satisfaction as he noted how well the clips were doing their job. He gave each a little tweak and Babala felt the slight thrill of pain draw down to her cunny, and this seemed to make her pout her mound higher as if in offer. 'Some girls struggle and I am forced to strap their hands to the back of the chair as well as fix their ankles in the stirrups. Most aggravating.' He frowned. 'You will not force me to do that, will you, my dear?'

Babala shook her head vigorously, making her golden curls tumble about her shoulders.

'Excellent. I think you are ready for the balm. It is my own recipe of fragrant herbs and spices and exotic unguents. It soothes the path of my cock, you understand, and makes you very amenable.' He paused, the pot ready in his hands, and smiled at Babala. 'Not that you aren't one of the most amenable girls I have had the pleasure to prepare.'

A shy smile curved Babala's lips at the compliment, but at the same time she felt a certain apprehension. What would this balm do to her cunny? She dared not lower her hands to hide her fleshpot or the master would think her wickedly disobedient like the other girls for whom he had no time.

Had she been able to move she would have trembled as the Taskmaster positioned himself between her spread thighs. He inspected her flesh leaves perhaps more minutely than was absolutely necessary, and remarked upon the contrast of the dark folds to the pinkness of her nubbin, erect and hard.

'Juices slick this delicate pot already,' he murmured, and Babala felt the quick lap of a tongue across the very point of her nubbin. 'There is nothing like the taste of a maiden, so fresh and sweet and yet so beckoning.'

Babala blushed at this and at the intimacy of the tongue kiss.

'No, no,' said the Taskmaster, rather crossly. 'Do not blush. I thought you were different from the other girls; innocent but willing.' He rewarded her with a finger slap upon her already tender breasts, but his anger quickly dissipated as he sniffed the open pot of balm.

An exotic perfume filled the room; more heady than those she perceived when she first entered it. It made her head swim and her fleshpot become more open and ready. She felt her sex leaves pout and swell and her nubbin grow, probing eagerly from its little hood. As the cool balm was spread into every crevice she felt her eyes close and her lips part. Her pink tongue-tip circled her lips very slowly in outright invitation, and the Taskmaster was quick to notice this, pressing his mouth against hers. She felt a smooth hardness caressing her eager cunny and teasing the still closed entrance. Her breath came softly, but quickly she realised it was his cock that nudged her entrance. It teased the cup of her fleshpot, mixing his own juices with hers that came in steady droplets, urged, no doubt, by the balm which made her cunny tremble and tingle.

'And how is that little nubbin now?' he asked, rather unnecessarily to Babala's mind, since he could surely feel her bud hot and throbbing against his cock, which he eased up and down, tickling the urgent tip of her core.

'It feels very ready, sir,' admitted Babala. 'It throbs and tingles unbearably.'

'Not unbearably,' said the Taskmaster, in a teasing tone. 'Is it not a delicious sensation? A sweet warmth which builds up in this little belly of yours?' The ball of his thumb pressed the bud in question, rubbing from side to side, but stopping just as Babala thought she would scream out her climax. He seemed to know instinctively how close she was to the brink, but he kept her hovering in tortured anticipation.

Babala was gasping in readiness. She could feel her maiden entrance pulsing with need and her nubbin jerked under every stroke of his thumb.

'I must now see the state of your pit,' he said. 'Just a quick inspection, you understand. Lift your bottom a little higher, my dear, so that I might touch the wrinkled bud.'

Babala closed her eyes in shy humiliation as his finger stroked the tightness, trailing back and forth over the tight pleats. She lifted her bottom higher and opened her eyes, just a fraction, saw him nod in satisfaction, and could not help the feeling of pride that washed over her. 'I shall leave the Prince to that delight,' he said, with another nod. 'And now, my dear...' He slicked his fingers up and down his cock and Babala noticed that the thickness was slippery with the same balm he had massaged into her fleshpot. She could not help but shiver, imagining the sensation this would cause within her.

'There will be no pain, my dear,' he promised in a husky whisper. 'Merely pleasure such as you have never known before. Feel free to scream, to thrust against me as your fleshpot opens like a flower in bloom as I pierce it.'

Babala's eyes were riveted to the vastly swollen globe that shone wetly in the dim light of the dancing candle flames. The length of the Taskmaster's cock and the ball of his globe seemed to increase as he approached her cunny with its stiffness. When the round smoothness actually touched her entrance she found herself butting forward to greet his thickness.

'Good, my dear,' he murmured, and kissed her once more, probing his tongue into her mouth. His fingers tweaked the silver clips and made her arch upwards, greeting his body, welcoming the intimacy. Her fleshpot seemed to spread itself to enfold his thickness. His length grated against her nubbin and she tried to murmur her pleasure, but his open lips muffled the sound.

There was no pain, only a mild feeling of being stretched open and her nubbin throbbing with delight. Again she tried to murmur, but was gagged by his lips and tongue. He drew back, and had her hands been free she would have held his broad shoulders to beckon him back deep into her cunny. Immediately he thrust deep inside her once more, his cock butting the very limits of her womb. Again and again he sank into her, making her delicate body shake with the force of his entrance. She felt her come draw up from the very soles of her straddled legs, felt his flesh slap heavily against hers and felt his crisp bush grate against the glossy wetness of her own curls.

Her freshly opened passage throbbed with pleasure and petted his thrusting length. His breath rasped in his throat and blew into her mouth, and then a fountain of heat sprayed her creamy passage walls and spilled outwards over her spread buttocks. Again and again he erupted into her as if he had never taken a girl before, and yet she knew the Taskmaster was the most potent of men in the castle. His job was to fuck all the maidens to prepare them for the Prince who was, in truth, a lazy indolent man...

Babala sighed in the chill of the cave. If only she was still in the arms of the Taskmaster, but she was not. She lay in the sand that formed the floor of the filthy cavern, and all these men had used her. The Lady Fazath seemed to sense that she was dreadfully unhappy and began to caress the softness of her breasts, the little swell of her tummy and the tender mound of her cunny.

'Can you never get enough of a girl?' demanded a rough voice, and at the same moment the Lady Fazath was kicked from Babala's arms.

'Leave her alone!' The mistress, although she must surely have been in pain from the kick, clung bravely to Capel's leg.

'Of course,' he growled sarcastically, 'the girl is yours, is she not?' Having freed himself from her he flung his huge body upon Babala, his rough hands gripping her whipped breasts, making her mew in pain. His cock butted at her cunny, thrusting between the tender folds and penetrating her passage.

'Haven't you done enough? You said you would take us back to the castle once you've had your fill of us,' whimpered the Lady Fazath, sounding nothing like her former warrior self.

'Nowhere near enough, my lady,' said Bart, his face contorted in an evil grimace. 'Nowhere near. I intend to change you from a wilful disobedient hussy to a womanly woman...' He looked over his shoulder to Babala, who was arching her body, offering it to Capel who gripped her buttocks the better to thrust into her fully. 'Peli, use the manacles and spikes to chain her ladyship to the wall. We'll take her one after the other. What you say, Graf?'

'Aye, use her roughly,' agreed Graf, 'front, back and in her mouth.'

'Use me,' begged Babala, her voice husky as she approached her orgasm. 'Do not taunt my lady any more. It is torture for her.' Her slender body shuddered with the force of Capel's thrusts. She knew the other men could see her naked breasts, their firmness quivering as the big man rutted against her; could see the tiny weals left by the tip of the lash; could see her swollen nipples, flushed scarlet from the rasping of Capel's tunic.

'No, no my sweet,' said the Lady Fazath, 'you have suffered enough.'

Capel rolled, sweating heavily from his exertions, from Babala's body. She could feel the heat of his cream trickling over her sex lips, seeping through the lushness of the golden pussy curls and slicking the dark flesh of her sex folds.

'Yes, you have suffered enough,' repeated the Lady Fazath. 'I shall do their bidding when...' she paused, and Babala could feel the heat of the woman's gaze on her slick and open cunny, 'when these brutes have allowed me to lick their come from your lovely body, from your cunny, from your rose-hole and from the sweetness of your mouth.'

The cave was silent except for the harsh and rapid breathing of the men. Bart spoke first, although Capel picked up his long whip and loomed over the two females, his face contorted with anger.

'Yes,' said Bart, holding up a warning hand, 'the woman suggests something which will be pleasantly entertaining; which will excite our appetites for what is to come.'

They meant to keep them prisoner forever, thought Babala. They would never let them go. She turned appealing eyes upon Peli, and he gave her a guilty answering smile.

'Get on with it!' growled Capel.

Lady Fazath needed no second bidding and, despite the cruel nature of her wounds, almost sprang to Babala's side, caressing her breasts and kissing the angry looking teats.

'Stop wasting time,' grunted Bart. 'Lick the little bitch.'

The mistress gave a smile and rose to her feet, hauling Babala's ankles over her own shoulders until the girl's cunny was close to her eager mouth, and then she licked her lips and drove out her tongue to pet the inner margins of Babala's swollen outer lips. As she licked she weaved her tongue back and forth to show the men how well she lapped their issue.

Transferring her attentions to Babala's inner lips she petted with her mouth, sucking the juices deep into her throat. Only then did she drive her tongue into the girl's entrance and the men heard the slurping as she sucked and licked.

'You were right, Bart,' grunted Graf, 'this is most entertaining.' His cock was again stiff and upright as he slicked his fingers up and down its girth. His balls were full and taut and Babala could see, even from her up-ended position, that he was close to his orgasm once more.

'Her bottom,' ordered Capel. 'I gave that a full measure.'

And he was not the only one, thought Babala; her rose-hole was no longer the virgin entrance that the Taskmaster intended. Lady Fazath eased apart her castigated buttocks to reveal the wrinkled rosebud, and Babala gasped as the woman opened the place and drove her tongue deep inside.

'We did not tell you to enjoy yourselves,' Capel spat angrily. 'You are doing this for our entertainment. Understand?'

With slicked lips the Lady Fazath smiled and bowed her head obsequiously. 'Of course, my masters. It is the girl who is at fault.'

Babala was aghast at this, and was hard pressed not to speak out in her own defence. She felt her breasts tremble as the Lady Fazath let her slide to the sandy floor of the cave.

'She cannot control herself so far as sexual pleasures are concerned.' The mistress sank down to the floor beside her and gave her a warning frown. 'She is an ill-disciplined hussy, which is why I was taking her from the castle. Such a bad influence on the other girls.'

It was then that madam fastened her lips upon Babala's, her tongue darting deep into her throat. Babala could taste her own cream and the bitter taste issued by the men, but this was nothing, was no punishment compared with the lies told by her ladyship.

The Lady Fazath had stolen Babala from under the Prince's very nose. The serving women were about to dress her in the jewelled gown but the Lady Fazath tossed the rich garment into a corner and made off down the maze of passages which led to the drawbridge and the castle grounds, with Babala slung like a sack over her shoulder.

'Lies,' murmured Babala, as madam took a gulp of air. 'That was not the reason. I was not a bad influence.'

'Be quiet, you little fool,' hissed the Lady Fazath. 'Be quiet.'

'Silence, the pair of you!' growled Bart, and Babala saw him take the long whip from Capel and swirl it above his head. She heard the whistle of it in the air and she felt her body tense, waiting for the cruel sting of it. 'Get away, witch!' he rasped, and it was the Lady Fazath who felt the cut of the leather.

Babala shrank away, hugging her arms about her breasts and crouching in the darkest corner of the cave. She heard madam whimper and heard the men laugh as they manacled her to spikes they had driven into the wall of the cave. Through the gloom Babala could see the spread-eagled form of her mistress. The strongly muscled legs were spread to their widest extent, the apex of them marked by the dark thatch of her pussy bush. Madam's arms, too, were widely spread, making her full breasts flatten upon her ribs and this served to make the teats stand out fully like dark brown nuts.

The men teased her ladyship with their lips and teeth, biting the hard and wrinkled nuts and sucking her cunny lips.

'A fine moist pouch of flesh,' grunted Capel, and Babala gasped as she saw her ladyship throw back her head. Surely it was pain that made her do this, and not enjoyment. Capel buried his lips between the pink sex folds, searching out the pert bud of madam's nubbin. 'And a dripping funnel,' he added, as he drew his mouth away and thrust two fingers deep into the open slit. He grinned cruelly as madam writhed on his probing digits, but whether this was in pleasure or distaste, Babala could not discern.

The other men, all except Bart, who so far as Babala could make out was the chief among them, took their turn at taunting the Lady Fazath. Capel, who teased her nubbin and thrust fingers into her depths, finished his humiliation of her by working his huge cock with his fingers and spraying madam's spread cunny folds with jet after jet of his issue.

'And how do you like that, your ladyship?' he grunted, as the creamy arcs splashed upon her flesh.

Babala peeped between her fingers, for she could not bear to witness her madam shamed in this manner, and saw that her ladyship had her head thrown back and her eyes closed.

Encouraged by the other men the young fellow, Peli, lifted his brief leather loincloth and approached the Lady Fazath. To Babala, who still peeped between her fingers, he seemed nervous as he drew back his foreskin to bare his swollen and shiny globe. It was as if he thought that madam was a magical creature who could make his cock shrivel and die.

'Go on, lad!' urged Graf, pushing the young man so hard that he fell upon madam's shamed body. 'What are you waiting for?'

'Shall we guide your cock in?' asked Capel with a cruel chuckle. 'I've greased the path for you.'

The other men laughed at this, and Babala saw the young man blush to the very roots of his hair. Tentatively, she crawled across the dusty floor of the cave. The men were so engrossed in their teasing of the Lady Fazath that they did not notice her until she reached Peli's feet and caressed his ankles. Looking up she could see the lad butt the globe of his cock at madam's vulnerable cunny. He frowned and gestured that she should crawl back to her hiding place at the rear of the cave, but it was too late.

'It seems the young filly is envious!' Bart exclaimed, and Babala whimpered with distress and pain as she was hauled roughly to her feet. She tried to protest but no words would come. She was not envious, simply sorry for the young man, feeling his humiliation as he was almost forced to take the Lady Fazath with his inexperienced cock.

'Well, my pretty?' rasped Bart. 'Do I understand correctly?' He held her close, lifting his leather skirt and brushing the thickness of his cock between her thighs, sawing it back and forth between cunny lips made slippery with the Lady Fazath's spittle.

'Yes, sir,' Babala lied softly. 'Yes, I am envious.'

'You want to feel the power of a cock within you?' Bart's voice was thick with lust. 'Opening you, pressing the soft cushions of your sex outwards, is that it?'

Perhaps, thought Babala, if she offered herself to the chief of these men they would stop torturing the Lady Fazath, release her from the manacles which she could see were making ankles and wrists raw.

'Yes, sir,' said Babala meekly. She hung her head, letting the golden cascade of her hair spill about each pale cheek.

'Then that is what it shall be,' said Bart, his words muffled against the softness of her neck, and a large rough hand cupped the underswell of a breast while the other slapped each thigh in rapid smacks until she opened her legs wide enough to his satisfaction.

'Have your fill of the woman,' he said, thrusting thick fingers into Babala's opening until she could not help but gasp at the force of it. She heard the other men grumble at their having to take second best, and she mewed miserably that her ploy had not worked.

'Come, my pretty,' said Bart, holding her prisoner. 'You and I will take our pleasure at the back of the cave.'

There was nothing Babala could do but submit, and to aid the man to take his fill of her. As his thickness drove into her she arched up to him, lifting his heavy body with her own slender one, and her mind drifted back to the Taskmaster, and his tenderness as he broke her virgin maidenhead. The memory took away the roughness meted out by Bart, and her climax was swift and endlessly pleasurable.

Chapter 3

Early the next morning Babala awoke feeling stiff and weary, and her cunny felt raw from its rough treatment. Her breasts were sore by days of less than gentle handling and her belly, buttocks, thighs and back were covered with welts, some fresh and red and others fading.

While the guards still slept she crawled to the entrance of the cave. In the pale dawn light mists moved like wraiths over the valley below. She saw, just a short distance away, a small lake as blue as her sapphire eyes. Although she was naked and shivering in the early morning chill she longed to immerse her aching limbs in the icy water.

With an apprehensive look over her shoulder at Bart, she edged close to the rim of the cliff in which the cave was situated. He was deeply asleep, mouth open and leather loincloth pushed to one side to reveal a cock, which even in sleep was stiff and upright, its globe bare and slick with issue. He smiled as if he dreamed of impaling Babala, and his forefinger and thumb rested at the base of his thick stem, pulsing the fleshy shaft.

The other men were similarly unconscious, weary from their sexual labours. Lady Fazath, drooping in her bonds, was suspended from the manacles driven into the cave wall. Babala felt a twinge of sympathy for the woman, but had she not brought all these troubles upon them by stealing the Prince's prize?

Babala sighed as she thought of the comfort and sensual delights of the palace, of her tender taking by the Taskmaster, and the waiting to be called from the harem to the presence of the Prince. That waiting made her belly liquid with joy and her sex moist with excitement.

The first rays of the sun appeared over the far horizon and Babala knew she must hurry if she was to experience the luxury of cool, refreshing water in her hair and enveloping her body. The chill would surely soothe her many wounds as well as slake her thirst.

As she turned to make her way down the short stretch of steep mountain she dislodged a stone, which tumbled noisily down the slope. She clung to the crumbling cliff face, her body tense, fearing reprisal from the guards if they should wake and catch her. She looked back once more to check them, but Bart merely grunted and turned on his side, still cradling his cock and thrusting into his dream woman.

It was not far down the mountainside, but the stones chafed Babala's bare feet as she scrambled to the bottom. She was oblivious to the pain, so anxious was she to soak the filth of the guards from her skin and hair and soothe the many abrasions that marred the previous perfection of her body.

At last she reached the foot of the cliff and ran swiftly along the short path that led to the lake. With a soft laugh of joy she dived into the icy water, cutting it like a knife with her perfectly arched body. It was bliss to feel the water cleansing her hair, washing away the dust from the cave and the evidence of the guards. Spreading her legs and using her fingers to open her sex folds she allowed the water to seep into her cunny. She dipped her head and took draught after draught of the cold water, drinking it down.

Lifting her hands she scrubbed her scalp. Water dripped from her breasts and shimmered like diamonds in the rising sun.

At last satisfied that her hair was clean she sank down beneath the surface of the lake again, allowing the golden cascade to float behind and above her. The chill of the water soothed her sore skin, cleansed the many hurts the men had inflicted upon her, and she closed her eyes, drifting languidly.

So lost in the ecstasy of this small luxury was she that she did not see a dark shadow casting narrowed eyes over her from the edge of the lake. It was a shock, therefore, to feel the sharp pain in her scalp, and it was as if her hair would be pulled out at the roots as she was dragged to the surface.

'Try to escape, would you?'

Babala was pulled from the lake by her hair. Her slender body, so recently cleansed by the water, was hauled through the mud at the edge and was streaked with dark earth.

'No - ouch!' she squealed, her fingers clawing uselessly at the hands that were wrapped around her long fall of wet hair. 'I was bathing!'

Plaintively, she looked up at Bart's coarse features, tears of pain coursing down her cheeks.

'Liar,' he grunted, and he slapped the still tender heaviness of her breasts. Babala dared not pull away, for she knew she would be punished further if she did. 'You were planning to run back through the forest, to tell the Prince what mischief we have enjoyed with you and the Lady Fazath.'

With tears of pain blurring her vision Babala ventured a look into his dark eyes, and her own widened with surprise for she could see much more than anger in them. Much more. There was fear plainly written on his coarse features; a twitch at the corner of his mouth, the eyes looking furtively this way and that, the nostrils wide as he breathed rapidly as if gasping for breath.

'No,' she managed. 'I merely came to the lake - '

She got no further, for the breath was wrenched from her body by Capel's whip snaking about her slender waist. 'Lying bitch!' he growled. 'They're all the same, these women. Can't wait to fuck and tell.' The whip snaked over her shoulder, knocking her to the ground, rolling her in the squelching mud.

'You came to wash, did you?' It was Graf's voice, growling and peevish. 'Look at you, you filthy whore. Breasts streaked with mud...' He rolled her over and she looked up at the three men, choking back sobs. 'Somehow it has even slithered here!'

The other men laughed as Graf slapped some of the thick dark mud upon her inner thighs, spreading her legs wide and smearing the filth in a thick cake within her cunny.

'We shouldn't be doing this...' it was Peli - nervous, timorous, trembling. 'We've been gone from the palace for five days. There'll be punishments waiting for us, I'll warrant.'

Graf, on his knees beside Babala, smoothing her body with the dark slime, shrugged, uncaring. 'We'll say they struggled and it was necessary to punish them, to restrain them until they learned how to behave.' He pinched her muddy nipples until she whimpered, and when she mewed in pain he slapped her belly, her breasts, enjoying the slurping sound of his hands on her muddy flesh.

'Peli is right,' Bart said with a nod, confirming the fear Babala had seen in his eyes. 'Do you think the Taskmaster will not be ordered to use his skill to test here and here?' He bent down beside Graf and probed his fingers between Babala's flesh leaves, opening them out, thrusting two muddy fingers into her cunny. That done he flipped her over and spread her buttocks to thumb the wrinkled bud of her anus, feeling the fresh give of the opening. 'He will know and we'll be punished severely.' He paused, lifting her bottom and spreading her legs as if he was enjoying the sight of these pretty parts for the last time. 'Maybe even executed.'

'Then we'll get rid of the bitches,' said Capel. 'I'll throttle them with my whip.' He wiped a dew of sweat from his forehead and his eyes seemed to burn as he gazed at Babala. It was as if she could see within his mind, could see herself lying helpless on the muddy ground beneath him, sinking into the slime as he wound the supple whip about her throat. 'Then we'll throw their bodies into the lake,' he added viciously.

'The lake isn't deep enough,' said Bart. 'They'd be found.'

A keening sound whispered over the scene. It was Peli, rocking back and forth, his uniform streaked with mud, his face contorted with fear and misery. 'What are we to do, Bart? What?'

'I don't know, lad.' He sat on a rock, his head in his hands. 'We can't take them back to the palace, but murder isn't the answer.' He raised his eyes and shook his head as he looked at Capel.

Babala shivered in the mud, her raised buttocks quivering with cold and fear as she wondered what fate awaited her with these men. She placed her hands on her head, indicating that she was entirely at their mercy - submissive and willing to do whatever pleased them.

'Ah!' Graf rose to his feet. 'The maid has given me an idea.' He grabbed Babala's arm, and the mud squelched as he pulled her to her feet. Filth splashed from her breasts and spilled onto Graf's leather tunic, so he gave her a sharp slap on the buttocks with his free hand and then continued as if there had been no interruption. 'There is a slave auction at the town of Brentasi, just over the border in the next kingdom.'

'Put them in an auction?' Bart's eyes brightened and he jumped to his feet, no longer fearful, but full of enthusiasm for this new adventure. 'That would solve all our problems and we could return to the palace to say they'd been taken by bandits. There are many around Brentasi.'

Could Babala's fate have been any worse, she wondered, had bandits taken her? 'If we are going to Brentasi,' she said shyly, her hands held tightly on her head, 'may I bathe once more in the lake?'

'And escape?' grunted Capel, shaking her so roughly her breasts swayed.

'She'll fetch a better price if she is clean,' observed Peli, and Babala glanced at him gratefully.

'True,' said Bart, with a nod. 'Lead her to the lake, Capel.'

A fierce grimace contorted the guard's face as he narrowed his cruel eyes at Bart. 'Aye, if you so order it, master,' he acquiesced tightly, 'but she'll not escape.' He twisted the supple leather of his whip about Babala's upper arm and half-pushed and half-pulled her to the lake. 'This madam will fetch many gold pieces I'll warrant, and we'll share the takings, eh?'

The other men grunted their agreement as they watched Babala dipped to the point of drowning into the icy cold water.

While Graf, Bart and Capel laughed at Babala's feeble struggles, Peli was sent to release the Lady Fazath from her chains.

She glared at him as he entered the gloom of the cave, and spat at him as he approached her.

'Where's Babala?' she demanded.

'Bathing,' said the lad, somewhat nervously. 'You're going to auction, both of you.'

Fazath did not fight the boy as he released the manacles. A plan was forming in her sharp mind. When the chains fell loose from her tired and naked body she almost fell into Peli's arms, so stiff was she from her long bondage.

'Auction?' she whispered, as pain took the breath from her body and the muscles regained their blood flow. 'What auction?' Her legs would not support her and she knelt at Peli's feet, her lips level with his scarcely clad cock.

'At Brentasi,' he said. He could feel the woman's breath close to his thickening stem. 'T-two days journey from here.' Soft lips took his globe within and he gasped with pleasure, but as suddenly as his knob was enclosed it was released, and his eyes flashed wide open with disappointment.

'If I suck your cock and drink down all your come,' Fazath cooed seductively, 'will you let me go?' She brushed her black hair against the lad's belly and her cheek against the smooth stiffness of his cock. Looking up at him she gave a winning smile and felt his shudder at her caresses.

'Graf and Capel said you did not enjoy the attentions of men... only women.' He croaked the words, fearful that the others should discover them, and yet his groin was aching with renewed fullness. 'And what of Babala? Would you leave her and allow my friends to put her up to auction?'

Fazath snaked her tongue around the lad's globe, allowing the very tip to tickle the pulsing single eye, and did not speak until the young man was trembling with her attentions. 'Will you let me go?' she said, clutching his muscular thighs. 'Will you?'

If she could only escape perhaps she could yet rescue Babala and spirit her away to some humble retreat in the forest, where she could delight in the luscious girl forever. Meanwhile, she must degrade herself and suck the youth for all she hated it, hoping she could then run.

'Do it,' rasped Peli. 'Do it. My cock is throbbing as if it would burst.'

Fazath, her midnight hair tumbled and matted by the days and nights of her trials, her body naked and grimy, arched her body backwards. Her full breasts pouted invitingly and she shuffled open her thighs to display the black nest through which flushed pink folds peeped. Peli groaned.

'Do you promise?' she whispered.

Peli's fingers rested at the root of his cock, trembling, aching to finish the pleasuring the woman had started. 'I'll do what I can,' he hissed, 'but do it or my balls will surely burst.'

With a laugh Fazath opened her mouth and engulfed the full length of the pulsing thickness. Her tongue snaked around the smooth tautness of his skin and her hands cupped his balls, massaging them gently as she used the pad of her thumb to play the sensitive spot between them and his anus. She heard him groan with pleasure and almost gagged as he thrust deeper and deeper into her throat.

Neither heard the tumble of stones as feet and hands clawed their way up the tortuous slope of the mountain. It was only when a growl of anger filled the cave that they realised they had been discovered.

But Peli was unable to stop his vigorous thrusting, reaching the point at which he was unable to stop. A moan of pleasure came from his throat and his spume gushed like a fountain into Fazath's throat, coating her tongue, her teeth, the soft inner lining of her cheeks.

'Well now, young fellow,' Graf's deep voice was punctuated with laughter. 'I came to rescue you from this harridan, but it would appear...'

Peli staggered back, tugging at his leather skirt, tucking it around his wilting cock and his balls. 'She - she was enticing me to help her escape!' he blurted. 'Without the girl!'

Like a panther Fazath sprang at the lad, her nails attacking him like claws, every muscle tensed in anger. Her well-developed biceps, recovered from their long bondage, bulged as she threw her arms around the lad's chest, crushing him until there was no breath left in him, and her calves wrapped about one of his as she threw him to the ground, where they rolled locked in combat.

'A pleasing sight,' grunted Graf, and Fazath heard the lust in his voice, knowing, even in battle, that men found her toned body enticing. 'But the time for play is over,' he added.

A hand stronger than hers prised her arms from the lad and held her, helpless as a kitten. Peli lay on the ground, gasping for breath while Fazath was mauled between her thighs with fingers that opened her cunny and thrust deep into the moist, yielding depths.

'Let me go!' She hissed the words.

'Fetch the cords, lad,' said Graf, never halting the crude invasion of her body. 'We shall have to tame this wildcat before we take her to Brentasi. Truss her up like a chicken.'

'No one will want me at the auction,' said Fazath. 'No one. They want girls like Babala.'

Graf crushed her to him and she could feel his thickness between her thighs. 'You're a handsome woman, Fazath, for all your maturity and your strange taste in sex. Someone will bid for you.' His mouth claimed hers, his tongue driving between her teeth as one hand kneaded the firm flesh of her breast and rolled a teat until she murmured in pain.

'What's this?' Bart's voice cut through the sudden silence in the cave. 'Must I do everything myself?'

Flung from Graf, Fazath was thrown to the floor and Peli stood over her with hanks of rope looped about his hands, looking nervously from one to the other of his superiors.

'The woman struggled,' said Graf. 'I was helping Peli to truss her. She can't be trusted not to run without full bondage.'

'Then do it!' barked Bart. 'I can't trust Capel with the girl. I have to return to the lake to watch him like a hawk. The man has a cruel streak which strikes a chill in my very bones.' He turned quickly and they could hear him hurrying down the shale on the mountainside.

'Loop her neck, Peli,' ordered Graf.

'But won't she choke?' Peli hesitated with the rope trembling in his hands.

Fazath was tempted to use all her strength to throw herself once more at both the men. She gritted her teeth and clenched her fists, trying to control her anger. What tortures was Babala suffering with that animal, Capel? What had they done to her? She was too passive - too submissive. Fazath shuddered at the thought of her beautiful girl in the clutches of that brute Capel.

'Only if she's stupid and struggles,' said Graf, after a pause in which he sneered at his captive. He cupped one of her breasts, caressing the lower swell and thumbing the teat again. Fazath bore the humiliation with gritted teeth, thinking of Babala. 'Make a noose, lad, slip it over her head and let the excess hang down her body.' The sneer became a grin, leering and lustful, as he watched Peli form a loop and, somewhat anxiously, slip the hemp rope about Fazath's neck.

As the rough cord abraded her skin and the noose was tightened, she swallowed hard and painfully. The rest of the length swung between the deep valley of her breasts, rasping first one and then the other. As she took many rapid and shallow breaths the rope dangled against her taut belly and brushed the triangle of blue-black pussy hair. She felt humiliated and used by the men and despised herself for being so pliant, but she was so for Babala, hoping they would use her more kindly.

'Hold your wrists together,' ordered Graf, still grinning. 'Grab her elbows, Peli,' he added over his shoulder. 'I don't want any bruises marring my handsomeness.' He let out a loud guffaw at his own wit, but the laughter faded as Fazath gave him a threatening glare.

Cruelly, he tugged on the rough rope, pulling it tight about her neck and wrapping it around her wrists. She winced as it rubbed against the wounds left by the manacles and gave several feeble coughs as she tried to catch her breath.

'Now down over your belly and between those sex lips,' he said, an evil chuckle punctuating his words. 'It will tickle that nubbin of yours and become wetted with your juices in no time.' He slapped her inner thighs apart with one hand while taking his time in positioning the cord between her sex folds so that it would rub her clitty at the slightest movement. 'And now,' he added, sliding behind her and making sure his cock probed between her buttocks, 'feel how deliciously prickly it feels against your bottom bud.'

Fazath made a feeble attempt to struggle against his attentions, and blushed as she admitted privately that the strands of the cords stimulated her rear opening.

'And finally...' the rope was twisted around her slender waist, lying against the swell of her hips. 'Of course, we must leave your feet free from bonds until we reach the auction. We don't want to tire ourselves by carrying you. We'll save our strength to spend the takings of your sale in the tavern.' Again he let out a loud guffaw before pushing Fazath towards the cave entrance.

The way out of the cavern seemed perilously steep, and she tried to turn her head, pleading for help from the two men, but only succeeded in half-choking herself.

At the foot of the steep slope she saw Babala, water streaming from her golden hair and shimmering on her pale skin. Her hands were bound but otherwise her body was free from bonds. The sapphire eyes widened when she saw her mistress and she opened her lips to protest, but Fazath gave an almost imperceptible shake of her head, warning her to hold her tongue.

The town square of Brentasi was thronged with onlookers; mostly peasants come to bring their produce to the market, but some to watch the auction of slaves, which was always good for an hour's entertainment. The crowd grew bigger as hundreds more entered the square.

They were roughly clad in brief tunics which, as they balanced the baskets of fruit and vegetables upon head or hip, rode up to bare their unfettered genitals. The girls and men alike took the opportunity to fondle each other. Slender feminine fingers ringed stiffened cocks while stout fingers, rough from farm work, slipped into warm and willing cunnies.

And it didn't end there. The day was hot and it heated the blood. Several couples sank to the cobbled square, the girls with their thighs parted and the men impaled within them. There was nothing like the auction to stimulate a good fuck.

Babala, tired from the two day march to the town and what had gone before, looked dully at the scene. Even the sounds of couples grunting their pleasure did not arouse her interest, although she heard the excited murmurs of the crowd as she and the Lady Fazath were pushed roughly into the square by the guards. Hands reached out to feel her naked breasts and went further, pushing between her thighs to stroke her fleshpot.

'You can't afford that one,' said Bart, giving the perpetrator of the intimacy a sharp blow on the shoulder with his whip. 'Don't touch.'

'And this one?' said the peasant, cupping Fazath's breasts and not at all put out by Bart's rebuke. 'She looks well used. Maybe I could afford her.'

His companions sniggered and gathered round to join in the fun, their hands reaching between Fazath's thighs, feeling the rope that had buffed between her sex lips for these two long days. They remarked how saturated the cord was, how hard her clitty had become, how deeply the bond had cut into the valley between her bottom cheeks.

'Enough of this!' growled Capel. 'Bid for the woman if you want her, but we warn you, she's a wild cat.'

As if to confirm this Fazath made a flying leap with both feet, knocking two of her tormentors to the cobbled ground of the square.

The Slavemaster, hearing the disturbance and noting the two spectators dragging themselves to their feet from the blow, was quick to leave the podium and stride to the scene. In his hand he held a long whip; leather, softened from years of usage. The handle was intricately carved and bulbous at the end.

'What is all this?' he demanded, the whip cracked ominously, and he eyed her up and down, noting the fading marks on her breasts and belly. 'Are these women for the auction?' He used a finger and thumb to inquisitively grasp one of Babala's nipples and lift her breast. She whimpered at the action, but held her head high and gave him a defiant stare.

'Yes,' said Bart. 'We've walked two days to get here. Is there space?'

The Slavemaster used the handle of his whip to trace the dip of Babala's waist and the luscious curve of her hip. 'Are they obedient? Arch your body, girl, so I may inspect your sex.'

'Very obedient,' Graf said quickly. 'As you can see, sir.'

The Slavemaster grunted and used the folded whip to probe between Babala's thighs.

'She should fetch a good price, sir, eh?' said Bart eagerly.

The Slavemaster used the bulb of the handle to open Babala's sex purse to its fullest extent. He thrust it back and forth within her and thumbed the tip of her clitty. 'She's been well used,' he decided. 'Very well used, and her skin is marked by the lash.' He turned to the men, but did not halt the thrust of the carved wood within Babala. 'Are you sure she's obedient?'

'You can see how willing she is, sir,' said Graf.

'Maybe too willing,' said the Slavemaster, noting Babala was in the throes of a gentle climax she could not control. The whip handle was pulled from her body unceremoniously, and Babala hung her head in shame at being so easily pleasured before the rough crowd.

'Still,' he conceded, 'perhaps some merchant will take her for his plaything. One never knows how these auctions will go.'

'I'm sure she'll fetch a mountain of shekels,' persuaded Bart.

'Really?' The Slavemaster raised a quizzical eyebrow. 'Well, I am not. And as for this harridan...' He gave an ironic smirk as he turned to the Lady Fazath. 'Well-developed muscles,' he commented, squeezing Fazath's biceps. 'Is she, perchance, of military background? She could be of use in Brentasi's guard.' He used his whip to part the woman's buttocks and to examine her rear hole. 'But perhaps not,' he concluded, answering his own statement as he fingered the opening to knuckle depth. 'This has been overused. A military woman would fight for all she was worth to preserve that chastity.'

The men looked at each other sheepishly and gazed down at their feet, shuffling them uncomfortably in the market debris.

'Why is she bound so?' asked the Slavemaster, fingering the rope that went from Fazath's wrists, down over her belly, pressing into the fleshy pad of her pussy mound, causing it to tighten about her neck and over her belly. Fazath coughed, but her expression was far from plaintive; rather her anger was plainly marked on her features and she hissed between gritted teeth at her tormentor.

'A wild cat,' commented the Slavemaster, but showed no concerns as he inspected her sex, easing the rope to one side and fully parting her sex folds.

'Careful, sir,' warned Bart. 'She's lithe on her feet.'

'I noted the disturbance among the crowd,' said the Slavemaster, but did not halt his inspection. 'A good length on the clitoris,' he commented, as he pushed back the hood to bare the tip. 'That's always a favourite with the women who delight in their own kind.' He continued to roll the slip of skin back and forth, thumbing the tip as he did so. Fazath grated her pubis in a rhythm that matched his attentions and Babala noted that her mistress's eyes became heavy about the lids.

When he was satisfied the woman was close to her climax he stopped, giving Fazath's cunny a pat as he did so. 'Yes, she will be greatly sought after by certain women.'

'Finish it, you fiend!' hissed Fazath, her dark eyes flashing wildly. She tugged at the rope, trying with all her might to reach her cunny with her bound fingers, but she only succeeded in tightening it about her neck.

'But you will want to be in a state of heightened sensuality, my dear,' said the Slavemaster, 'to persuade the prettiest of women to buy you, will you not?'

'Let me!' Babala exclaimed, throwing herself at her mistress's feet. 'Let me help her. Let me bring her to her climax.' The Taskmaster had warned that her kind nature and willingness to please could get her in trouble, but Babala's soft lips were parted and her tongue-tip protruded between her white teeth. 'She has been tortured by these - '

The crack of the whip echoed above the babble of the crowd and Babala was lifted off her feet by the force of the blow as it snaked about her waist. The guards looked on in astonishment. Capel, in particular, narrowed his eyes in envy at the skill the Slavemaster demonstrated with his whip. Babala, the breath sucked from her body by the tightening of the supple leather around her waist, found herself looking into the cold grey eyes of the Slavemaster, for the coils of the whip had drawn her close to him. She could feel his cock hardening under the richness of his satin robe, embroidered in silks to depict all manner of lewd scenes, and it made her more aware of her own nakedness and vulnerability.

'How dare you presume to even suggest help for that woman.' His voice was low, hissed in her ear. 'You are a slave. Don't you understand that? And by the looks of things, born to be one.' Babala felt his fingers opening her sex, slicking them through her moistness, and rubbing her nubbin in rhythmical strokes. 'Answer me,' he whispered huskily, 'or am I to add dumb insolence to the rest of your crimes?'

The sweet heaviness of limbs came upon Babala, that which she was taught to enjoy by the Taskmaster. Breasts swelling and nipples hardened to taut buds, she leaned against the Slavemaster. 'Yes, sir,' she murmured. 'I am insolent. I deserve whatever punishment you give me.'

'You do not deserve this,' he rasped as his hand wormed between her thighs. 'You know that, don't you?'

'Yes, sir,' Babala whispered. 'I am aware of that.' It was as if she was mesmerised by the heat of his body, the smell of his masculinity, and she gave an involuntary gasp as strong fingers entered her, slipping into her warm moistness.

Everything around her; the Lady Fazath, the guards, the noisy crowds, were as nothing as she pleasured herself on his skilled fingers. Using the muscles of her sex she petted them and moved her hips in a rhythm that matched his hand. At every inward thrust he chafed her clitty and she could not hold back her mews of pleasure. It did not occur to her that she was writhing like an animal in a very public place; she was merely doing what she had learned from the harem and the Taskmaster.

'A pity the girl is so used,' he sneered derisively as he pushed her away from him, and she hung her head in shame as she staggered, buffeted and surreptitiously mauled by the encroaching crowd. She was disgraced, but even so, something in his eyes told her that he was not dismissing her so lightly as it seemed. He fingered the silken tresses of the cascade of golden hair, stroked the taut underswell of her breasts, and released the leather whip from her waist in an almost tender manner.

'Had she not been so marked and her body so penetrated by cocks from goodness knows where,' he said, as if speaking to himself, 'she would have fetched a pretty price.'

'How much?' asked Bart, his eyes eager and bright.

'Oh, easily a casket full of shekels, but as it is...' He turned away, but beckoned over his shoulder to the guards. 'Bring them to the podium. We'll see what we can get for you.'

Babala was pulled through the sniggering crowd by her bound wrists. Hot tears stung her eyes. The Slavemaster enjoyed her, that much was plain, but then threw her from him like a used dishrag. For the first time in her life she felt shame in her talent for giving pleasure to men. Even the guards had not made her feel so humiliated, for all their cruelty and taunting.

As she stumbled through the square, led by Bart, men lifted their tunics and thrust out their cocks lewdly. Women spat at her and spread their thighs, arched their hips, or stuck their fingers between their sex lips, pushing them in and out like cocks.

'Whore!' spat one woman.

'Harlot!' hissed another.

Helpless though she was in her almost total bondage, the Lady Fazath gave a few well-placed kicks, scattering the bullies like dominoes falling one after the other. Babala lifted her head just enough to give Fazath a look of gratitude.

At last they reached the podium. Graf, Capel, Bart and Peli positioned themselves as close to the small stage as they could. The other girls waiting to be sold were clad in simple white gowns, which although flimsy, preserved just a little modesty. Looking at them surreptitiously Babala could not help the envy that twisted in her stomach. They looked so clean and neat, almost virginal, and even more, they had no marks left by the whip. Babala's cramped hands strayed to the latest welt, the one that spanned her waist from the Slavemaster's lash.

'We have an excellent parcel of slave girls for you this morning, ladies and gentlemen,' cried the Slavemaster. The babble of the crowd died to a soft murmur at his commanding voice. He pushed a slender dark-haired girl forward. Babala judged her age to be no more than her own.

'This one will make an excellent body slave for some discerning gentleman,' he continued and, as he spoke, he ripped the girl's gown to bare her breasts. They were pert, the nipples small, pink as a maiden's. 'These will fill out nicely with regular treatment,' he added, and patted each breast in turn, first with his fingers and then lifting the delicate curve of the underswell with the whip handle.

The girl blushed with humiliation and tried to gather the torn folds of her gown together to hide her breasts.

'Stop that!' ordered the Slavemaster. 'You are here to be shown, and do you think your new master will allow such false modesty?'

The crowd sniggered and the girl choked back a sob as the Slavemaster ripped her gown further, baring a flat belly that was adorned by a gold ring at her navel. From the ring were suspended two fine gold chains that were pulled to the girl's crotch, and Babala could see a glint of gold where the outer lips of her cunny split.

'This one has been kept chaste,' said the Slavemaster, with a meaningful look at Babala. 'She was properly brought up and her sex pouch has been kept unsullied by men. Her mistress kept her cunt behind this golden door.' He slapped the girl's inner thighs with the whip handle to indicate that she should spread them. 'Tilt,' he ordered brusquely.

Obediently, the girl did as she was told and the crowd's murmur grew as between the parted legs they saw a fitted gold cup, locked about the girl's body by the fine chains.

'Turn round,' he commanded, 'and bend forward, thighs kept nicely apart.' The girl, in her embarrassment, hesitated, although only for a moment. 'Do as you're told!' The crack of a palm upon a curvaceous buttock broke the sudden hushed silence in the market square.

Babala bit her lip as she heard sobs break in earnest and saw the girl's spread legs tremble as she bent forward. Again an excited murmur ran through the crowd. Between the parted buttocks could clearly be seen a gold padlock, positioned exactly at the girl's bottom hole.

'She must ask to be released for natural purposes,' explained the Slavemaster. 'Such a ploy keeps them subservient, you see, ladies and gentlemen.'

The girl was pushed to the very edge of the podium and her tattered gown was drawn from her shoulders to leave her completely naked. The Slavemaster ordered her to stand with legs apart and cunny tilted to display the chastity cup and the plump flesh lips that cocooned its sides.

'Head up and dry your eyes,' hissed the Slavemaster, chucking the girl under the chin with the whip handle. 'Look boldly upon the crowd and try to smile. Do you think your new master will enjoy a girl who weeps and is afraid when he approaches with his cock at the ready to open her maidenhead?'

Babala's guards were amazed at the number of shekels the girl fetched, and they looked enviously as she was taken away by her new owner, a large man with fierce eyes and a whip held ready in his free hand. The girl looked pleadingly over her shoulder at Babala, but there was nothing to be done. Nothing.

At last it was Babala's turn to be pushed to the front of the podium, and the Slavemaster was scathing in his remarks about her.

'A beauty, this one,' he said, 'but much used, I'm afraid, ladies and gentlemen. She is also marked by the whip, although she heals well.' He turned Babala round and tapped the round hillocks of her bottom to point out the paling welts. 'And here,' he said, turning her again to lift her breasts and stroke her belly. He tapped her again. 'Tilt to reveal your cunny, girl.'

Sapphire eyes wide with pleading, Babala shook her head almost imperceptibly, knowing that the Slavemaster's seed was still coating the golden curls of her outer lips.

'Tilt!' he snapped, slapping her breasts, so with legs tensed and parted Babala tilted her cunny forward as he demanded.

'Use your fingers to reveal yourself further.' His voice was low and his dark eyes hooded with lust as he gave the order.

It would do her no good to disobey, Babala knew that, so with trembling fingers she peeled open her outer lips. At the sight of the juicy folds and flushed pink nubbin the crowd gave a howl of glee that rose to a roar when the Slavemaster tapped the bud with the tip of his whip.

'A beautiful sight, ladies and gentlemen, is it not?' he said. 'This girl could become quite a conversation piece within your household.'

It was then that he began to push the bulbous knob of the whip handle into the slippery folds. 'But nothing is perfect,' he continued. 'She is well used here...'

Babala clutched the bulb with her cunny muscles to show that she remained tight, but the Slavemaster made no mention of it, simply turned her round roughly. 'And here,' he added, forcing her to bend, the whip handle bulb played about her rear hole.

'I do not expect you to pay a great deal for such used goods,' announced the Slavemaster, almost sorrowfully. 'She allowed herself to be used by rough soldiers and they were a little too playful, a little too boisterous in their usage.' He frowned at the guards, shook his head and tutted in a chiding manner.

The crowd was silent until one woman cried out, 'Whore!' and others took up the cry until the square was a hubbub of catcalls.

'Quite right, my dear ladies and gentlemen,' he said, grinning widely until the catcalls died down. 'Nothing but a whore, so I'll have her taken below and then send her to be used in the taverns.'

'What do you mean?' asked Bart. 'She gets nothing? Not a shekel?'

The Slavemaster shrugged as he handed her over to a jailer who stood at the back of the podium. 'I'm afraid so. Too used, you see.'

Babala hung her head in humiliation as the Slavemaster's helper stepped forward. 'Jailer,' he said, 'take her below until I have time to deal with her.'

The jailer was a filthy creature and Babala cringed as he clutched her upper arm with his grimy fingers. He wore a greasy square of leather to hide his genitals and his upper body was covered in dark matted hair.

'A whore, eh?' he hissed through broken, rotted teeth, as he dragged her from the podium and down a flight of worn steps to a maze of dark and dank cells.

'No, I'm not a whore,' Babala said, through sobs of indignation. 'I was prepared for the Prince.'

The jailer's filthy free hand slipped down over the pleasing flatness of her tummy to the pad of her pussy mound. 'And what Prince is that? There is no prince in Brentasi. Only a dictator.'

Babala twisted her body, trying desperately to escape his loathsome advances, but his fingers slipped down further to enter the moist crevice of her sex pouch. She felt his ragged nail stroke the slippery tip of her nubbin and she couldn't help but arch against his touch.

'And a well trained whore at that,' the foul brute croaked. 'You love the touch of a man, do you not? See how you thrust against my fingers, urging me to slip them into your warm softness.'

'It's because I was trained…'

'Just as I said; a well trained whore.' The jailer twisted her against him, lifting the leather square to reveal his cock, bigger even than Capel's. 'Not many girls can take this. They scream with horror at the thickness and length of it. I was cursed until the Slavemaster flung you to me.'

'I was trained by the Taskmaster in the palace of Ellipsis,' Babala insisted, but such was her training that she no longer struggled.

'Good…' he murmured. 'Excellent.'

She could feel the massive bulb of his flesh sword opening the dark folds of her cunny and her breathing became more rapid as her traitorous excitement grew.

'Perhaps you would like to play a little game.' The two were locked together by the gnarled length that was partially inserted between her thighs.

'As it pleases you, sir,' Babala whispered meekly. Her training went deep, and as the jailer said, perhaps she was too well trained for her own good.

'Oh, it would greatly please me,' he wheezed, and then pushed her to the darkest corner of a dank cell and she felt the hardness of wood against her bottom, and then she was lifted and placed upon a worn table-like contraption.

'What is this?' she asked fearfully, her buttocks lifted by a shaped wooden pillow that served to also part her thighs. She felt extremely open and vulnerable.

'As I said,' murmured the jailer, 'just a little toy of mine...'

Wrists released from the bonds Babala had worn for two days were immediately clamped wide apart in shackles fixed to the head of the table. Her ankles were similarly spread and clamped securely, and the position in which she was placed lifted her tummy and breasts and offered her fleshpot to her captor. She was rendered totally helpless and at the jailer's mercy.

The bottom pillow thrust up and spread her sex, and she was all too aware that the dim candlelight revealed her pert pink nubbin very clearly against the darkness of her sex folds.

'How do you feel?' The jailer bent to lap his tongue about each bud of her nipples.

'V-very open,' admitted Babala.

'As a whore should be for her client.' The tongue laid a trail of spittle over her raised belly and wetted the upper curls of her cunny.

'I'm not a whore.' Babala struggled against the iron clamps, but only succeeded in causing her wrists to be chafed by the cold hardness of the iron manacles.

'Who but a whore would allow herself to be led to this table so willingly?' persisted the odious jailer, shuffling between her straddled thighs. 'Eh? Answer me that.' He waved his monstrous penis over her like a huge wand. It was thick and full, the skin stretched by its contents, the bulb shining with the slime of pre-issue.

'The Taskmaster tutored me well,' Babala argued meekly, her eyes fixed upon the waving cock. 'I was taught to please men, but I am not a whore.'

The jailer grunted and slumped upon her helpless body, and her opening was so slick and ready that he entered her without trouble. A sigh of supreme pleasure whispered from his slobbering lips and Babala could feel him pulsing in her cushiony depths. She could feel him butting at the very limits of her womb, but remembering what the Slavemaster had said about her used condition, she clung like a limpet upon the jailer's cock and watched his eyes open in surprise.

'How beautiful!' he grunted, drool glistening on his unshaven chin. 'No woman has done that...' The crushed girl heard his foul breath quicken and become shallow as he shunted deep into her with rapid stabs. But despite his rough appearance she could not help the naughty thrills of pleasure that swirled in her lower belly; could not help the pouting of her breasts against his scrawny chest, the arching of her pussy mound against his butting groin.

'How now?' bellowed a familiar voice, becoming louder as the owner descended the ancient slimy steps to the cells. 'What is this?'

The jailer sweated heavily over Babala, wetting the tendrils of golden hair that spread about the smooth and creaking wood of the bench, and with a final pig-like grunt he thrust and released his jets of copious semen into her. He grunted again and struggled to pull his cock from her clutching depths, but when he did his still turgid cock continued to spurt, arcing its cream onto her belly and thighs.

'She - she tempted me, sir,' he blurted sheepishly, his greasy hair curtaining his bowed face. 'I could not help myself, sir.'

The newcomer laughed, stepping over to the bench and fingering the cold iron that manacled Babala's wrists. 'So I see.' The tone dripped sarcasm, and the richly woven and embroidered satin of the Slavemaster's robe rustled in her ears, and she knew that, despite his apparent merriment, he was angry. 'She clambered onto the rack and locked herself into the clasps herself, I suppose.'

'More or less, sir,' the hateful jailer confirmed, lacking the intelligence to concoct a more convincing lie of his own, whilst wiping his cock with the greasy square of leather that scarcely covered the thick length.

'Please, that's not true,' Babala protested, tugging in vain at the iron that shackled at wrists and ankles. She managed to arch her bottom from the carved wooden pillow, as if this would help to release her, and in the gloom she could see two more shadowy figures and hear the clink of chains.

'However, it is true,' said the Slavemaster, 'that you enticed the jailer to fuck you with his huge and filthy cock once he had shackled you to the rack. Is it not, my dear?' He idly slapped the fullness of her breasts as he pondered aloud.

'No,' Babala denied, rolling her head from side to side on the table, 'it isn't.'

'Really?' said the Slavemaster, a quizzical eyebrow raised. 'Then what of this?' With a look of distaste he trailed the handle of his whip through the spillage pooled on her flat stomach, and allowed some excess to drip in chilly trails upon her breasts.

'Stop that, you filth!'

Babala's eyes widened at the sound of the Lady Fazath's commanding voice, and widened still further at the sound of flesh slapping naked flesh.

'Mind your own business!' ordered a croaking voice. 'You're mine now and you have no right to tell the master what he can and cannot do. If you speak again I shall gag you until you can learn to hold your tongue.'

'That's the way to treat a disobedient woman, crone,' said the Slavemaster, with a chuckle.

'Unfasten the maid's shackles and wipe the filth of your issue from her,' he ordered the jailer, and then turned back to the old woman who clutched the Lady Fazath. 'And I wish you well with that one; a wildcat if ever I saw one.'

Chapter 4

Babala was placed in a cage much like that used to transport animals destined for the travelling circuses that roamed the lands around Ellipsis. Filthy from the stink of the jailer, she huddled in a corner of the cage, shivering with cold in her nakedness.

As she was prepared for her journey, manacled at feet and ankles, her new owner, the Slavemaster, had taunted her unmercifully.

'Well, I certainly got a prize in you, my dear, did I not?' he said with a triumphant grin.

'You tricked the guards,' she said meekly. 'By telling the buyers how worthless I was you gained me for nothing.'

The whip snaked out and lashed the rounded hillocks of Babala's bottom, leaving a bright stripe of scarlet on her pale flesh. 'Insolence! That is what you get for insolence and, no doubt, my servants will delight in giving you more of the same.'

Babala hung her head, but whispered, 'Where are you taking me?' The flesh of her bottom burned and she knew that each buttock would be flushed while the long welt would be swollen, standing proud and dissecting the twin globes.

The Slavemaster pulled her to him and she could feel the blessed coolness of his satin robe against her whipped rear. She could feel his cock, stimulated to thickness and length, pressing into her heated flesh. 'Up there,' he said, pointing to a high crag.

The sapphire eyes were drawn to the place to which the Slavemaster pointed. The distant castle was dark and brooding, with many turrets and meandering castellated walls, and seemed to be perched perilously on the crag.

'But how will we reach it?" she asked.

The Slavemaster lifted his robe and Babala could feel his cock butting between the burning and rounded hillocks of her bottom. 'There is a way,' he said thickly. 'The carriage is well sprung and my horses are surefooted.'

A slick and silky globe butted at her rear hole, forcing the tightness to open, and the glow from the lash of the whip seemed to increase as he thrust his length into her. His hands cupped her fleshpot, massaging the soft pad, fingers opening it and entering between the folds. They slithered in the wetness left by his cock and that of the jailer's. They slid over the hard point of her nubbin, making Babala tremble with pleasure.

'How delicious you find it, my dear,' he murmured, lifting the silken tendrils of her hair to whisper in her ear. 'And this...' he pushed deeper into her rear entrance, making her moan, partly in pain and partly in ecstasy. 'Come for me, my dear girl. Let me feel your bottom clutch my cock as you shudder with delight.'

Babala flung her head back to rest upon his shoulder, her eyes closed, her lips parted and moist. Fingers squeezed the soft fullness of her breasts, tweaked each nipple until tears spilled down her peachy cheeks.

He pushed deeper.

'I am so grateful to the man who opened this tight ring of yours,' he murmured. 'So very grateful. Used you might be, but used deliciously.'

'Th-the guards used me,' admitted Babala, her tones hushed. 'They were sent to return the Lady Fazath and me back to the palace, but they kept us imprisoned in a cave for days.'

'I know,' he whispered. 'And fed you on their come, no doubt.'

'Yes,' gasped Babala as he began to work his cock slowly in and out. 'And very little else, sir.'

'In the kitchens... at my castle... you will be fed handsomely,' he grunted, his breath rasping as he fingered the silky wetness of her cunt and butted hard into her bottom.

'Oh, thank you, sir,' she murmured, having difficulty in holding back the spasms of bliss which rippled through her body.

'Providing... you do as you are told by my cooks.' Laughter lurked in his throat, Babala could tell, even though he sped to his orgasm. She felt him pump into the darkness of her bottom, his cock throbbing against her own spasms. Her nubbin pulsed under his fingers and juices seeped from her cunt as it, too, squeezed in and out.

'I - I am to work in the kitchens, sir?' she panted. She was beginning to suspect that the Slavemaster felt some concern for her and what she had suffered at the hands of the guards.

'Where else?' He pulled from her. 'And if you say a word to my wife about what we have done...' He looked to the peak of the crag. 'Well, you would not be the first girl to be hurled to the rocks below.'

Thus, naked and shivering, Babala was thrown into the cage while the Slavemaster wrapped himself in furs against the chill of the high peaks and the night, before making himself comfortable in the deep leather seat of the carriage.

'What is this place?' asked the Lady Fazath, her limbs aching after days of being bound in the coils of hemp rope.

'My cottage,' said the crone. Using a knife that glinted in the firelight and was held just a little too close to Fazath's skin for comfort, the wizened creature cut the bonds that noosed about her neck and wrists.

The relief was almost as delicious as an orgasm that had been a long time coming, and Fazath moaned with the pleasure of it. The crone cackled and reached to cup each of Fazath's firm breasts, and such was her relief from bondage Fazath did not pull away from the gnarled hands that had an amazingly smooth and sensual touch. The moans became more frequent and rhythmic and Fazath drew closer to the creature, for all she found her revolting in the extreme with her bent body, frazzled grey hair and wrinkled visage.

'Who are you?' she murmured, as her breasts were fondled in a disturbingly delightful manner.

'Does it matter?' croaked the harridan, slitting the rope around Fazath's waist and fingering the reddened mark the bondage had left. 'I bought you fair and square at a very reasonable price. The Slavemaster made it quite clear that your taste veered towards women.' One gnarled hand moved and slipped between Fazath's thighs to cup the full fleshpot that hid there. 'It didn't matter a jot to me that you'd been well used by men.' The bent fingers parted the fleshy leaves and slipped between them. Fazath arched her lithe body, giving the old woman free access to her cunt, moving with her as the fingers rubbed back and forth over the nubbin and feeling it grow under the touch.

'There,' croaked the crone, 'what a well-developed little bud. Let's see if we can lengthen it further by slipping back the hood.'

It did not seem at all strange to be fingered so intimately by this strange creature. The fingers were the most sensual Fazath had ever experienced, very knowing and skilled in the ways of women. Her nubbin had never felt so sensitive and yet the crone kept her hovering on the very brink of an orgasm, allowing her to anticipate it rather than to experience the full delight of it.

'Yes,' moaned Fazath, 'make me come.'

With a low cackle the harridan led her on legs that were barely able to support her, to a low cot spread with tumbled blankets, which might have been grey or green with mould for all Fazath cared in the ecstasy to which the woman had brought her.

'Spread your legs,' croaked the crone, 'and lift your knees. Let them fall outwards on the bed.'

'Aren't you going to bare yourself?' asked Fazath, somewhat tentatively. Why did she ask that question? The old woman looked bad enough in her tattered rags; the heavens only knew what she would look like naked. It was the hands that were so amazingly sensual - the fingers that applied just the right pressure at her most sensitive points.

The crone cackled as she crawled between Fazath's parted legs. 'When the time is right,' she said, 'and only then.' Once more, with fingers so soft that Fazath felt she wanted to scream at their sensuality, her flesh folds were spread open and her nubbin was cosseted to its full erect length. The hood was pushed back to its fullest extent, making the tip feel raw and exposed.

'*Yes...*' murmured Fazath, more urgently than before, but the crone kept her hovering close to her orgasm. It was amazing, she thought vaguely, that such an elderly person should have such patience and sexual knowledge.

It was when the tip of a skilled tongue flicked the raw tip of her nubbin that Fazath really whimpered. The spasms of delight rippled through her, but they were those of a pre-orgasm when the body feels heavy and lethargic, the breasts feel tender and swollen, juices wet the flesh folds and the female entrance flutters open.

'You are ready, are you not, my beauty?' croaked the crone.

'Oh, *yes*.' Fazath felt tears course down her cheeks. 'Won't you release me?'

'In good time.' The harridan bent her grey head and Fazath felt the coarse hair brush her open thighs, and even this seemed pleasurable to all her heightened senses.

The tongue flicked out again and snaked about the root of Fazath's nubbin, teasing the frill of fine skin that was the hood. It lapped at the tender tip, but stopped at the very moment when Fazath felt her orgasm rise up and begin to consume her with sensual fire.

'I can't stand it!' screamed Fazath. 'Please let me come!'

The crone licked her lips, savouring the musk of Fazath's juices. 'In good time.' The tone was more severe, almost masculine in its depth. 'Be patient,' the harridan added, the tone once more soft and cajoling. 'You cannot say you are not enjoying what I do to you.'

'No,' agreed Fazath. 'But it is torture!'

The crone laughed and the laughter seemed to echo about the small room. The sound seemed somehow familiar, but Fazath could not think from where.

'You are my slave,' she was reminded. 'I can do anything I wish to you. I can pleasure you, torture you, whip you, clamp those teats with devices which will keep you slavish for as long as I wish...' The crone pinched Fazath's nubbin, drawing the little hood back and forth in a way that was delicious torture. 'I can finger this...' the sensual fingers spread Fazath's buttocks to bare her bottom hole. 'Finger it, introduce the thickest phalli into its darkness...'

Fazath shivered.

'This, for example...' A white candle shaped like a huge cock, with a frighteningly thickened bulb at its end, was waved before Fazath's eyes. 'How does this excite you?'

Again Fazath trembled and yet at the same time her cunt pulsed with unbidden pleasure. Her bottom hole, too, clutched on the imagined wax phallus and she pressed against the crone's teasing fingers. 'Do it,' she pleaded. 'Do it all!'

A long drawn out howl of laughter came from the crone's throat and she bent once more to tease Fazath's open cunt. She slipped a filthy pillow beneath her buttocks, lifting her to make her more vulnerable, more open and revealed. Fazath groaned as her cunny lips were sucked in turn and pressed fully open. Soft lips engulfed her nubbin and palpated it in a pleasing rhythmic way.

She felt the great bulb of the wax phallus being twisted in the cup of her sex pouch, being coated with creamy juices. It was pushed deeply into her cunny and thrust in and out at the same time as her nubbin was expertly caressed with lips and tongue.

'I cannot hold back,' groaned Fazath, her toned body writhing against the tongue, lips, and the wax phallus.

'You can and you will,' ordered the crone, and the bulbous knob was pulled from her, still dripping with the copious juices she'd produced.

'Oh, *please*...'

'You plead after all the many times you have teased girls?' The crone's voice was deeper, threatening, and Fazath's dark eyes flashed open and her mouth dropped in surprise.

'How do you know that I...?'

The lubricated knob of the wax phallus was pressed at her bottom opening, stretching the tight muscle. 'Never you mind how I know. I just do. I know how you stole Babala.'

'I suppose the Slavemaster told you that,' said Fazath. The pressure at her rear opening increased, but she had to admit it was not unpleasant. It simply enhanced the sensations that came from her nubbin. The pressure became greater and Fazath moaned, but arched her back as if seeking greater stimulation.

'It will soon be in your bottom, my dear,' croaked the crone, who rubbed the soft open folds of Fazath's fleshpot with the heel of her hand as she drove the wet thickness of her tongue into her pulsing cunny.

Fazath's moans became louder and she butted her cunt against the crone's hands and tongue.

'There's my good little slave,' murmured the old creature. 'There's my good little sex slave. Now you know how those girls in the harem felt when you made them clamour for more of your attentions.'

How did she know that? But the question was fuzzy in Fazath's mind as the bulb slipped fully into her bottom and the thick wax phallus followed, increasing the pressure on her cunny and trembling nubbin. 'I'm coming,' she gasped. 'I cannot hold back any longer. Oh, it is so wonderful! Are you watching the throb of my cunny, the jerk of my clitty, how my opening sucks in and out? Is it as beautiful as it feels?'

'Indeed, my dear,' said the crone. 'Your cunt is performing deliciously. The nubbin is jerking just as it should. The folds flutter, and are deliciously swollen, much inflamed. Your opening is pulsing, waiting for a cock.'

The Lady Fazath's eyes, which had for many minutes been hooded with desire and heavy with lust, flickered open. 'A cock?'

'Yes, my love,' said the crone, with a deep throated chuckle. 'That which men carry between their thighs; that which thickens and lengthens when a woman seduces them...'

'Me? Seduce a man? Perish the thought!' She struggled to close her thighs. 'Never! Never has it been known.'

'And the guards in the cave?' asked the crone, and her voice sounded yet sterner; not at all womanly, but Fazath did not particularly notice that. She was too concerned with the fact that the crone knew of the awful days in the cave.

'You know about that?' She wished with all her heart she could hide her naked body while only moments ago it was delicious to display it to the full.

'You were followed,' said the old woman, her voice again ancient and cracked, 'you and Babala, from the time you left the palace and ran through the forest.'

'Oh,' groaned Fazath. 'You saw everything?' This old woman had seen how she and Babala had been humiliated and used by the guards; how she, Fazath, was held in restraints while the brutes took her one after the other.

'Not me, but one of my helpers.'

Fazath peered about the gloomy one room cottage. 'You have helpers? Employees?' The place reeked of poverty. In fact, Fazath wondered how the woman managed to purchase her at all.

'Oh, enough of this,' snapped the crone. 'We were talking about cocks. Men and the wonderful thickness they have between their thighs.' The old one sat on the edge of the cot and stroked the open folds of Fazath's sex pouch.

'Wonderful thickness?' Fazath grimaced.

'There were times when you enjoyed your bondage in the cave and what the men did to you. Isn't that true?' The gnarled fingers petted the creamy moistness between Fazath's thighs. 'And don't tell me you did not enjoy my wax phallus, because I know you did.'

'That's different,' said Fazath, with a pout. 'You are a woman and you played with my sex in a womanly way.'

'Are you sure?' The crone began to help Fazath from the cot, stroking each breast in a very sensual manner; a manner that made Fazath's eyes become heavy and the lids draw down over the dark orbs.

'What are you doing to me?' she asked huskily. 'What's happening to me?'

'Merely demonstrating that there is more than one sex...'

'I know that, you stupid old woman - '

Pain, like fire, shot through the muscular hillocks of Fazath's bottom. Again the pain whipped her fleshy mounds. So quickly did the whip fall that she had no time to cry out. Her buttocks burned as the whip cut across the full cushions of her bottom, and the breath was sucked from her body as the lash fell again and again.

'Must I remind you that you are my slave?' hissed the crone. 'You are mine, to be used as I wish.'

Rubbing her buttocks, Fazath bowed her head. 'You've made your point,' she said, although her words were far from meekly spoken, and then she raised her head and was shocked at what she saw.

The crone had thrown off her rags. The grizzled grey hair was gone and long dark locks fell to manly shoulders. The muscular chest was bare and tanned. The waist and hips were narrow and were thonged with a strip of fine leather from which hung a small square of cloth, heavily encrusted with jewels, and the skimpy garment was raised by the contents it scarcely hid.

'But... but you're a man!' Fazath gasped.

'Very much so.' The voice was no longer disguised, but was deep and rich.

'I know you...' Fazath tried to back away from the towering figure.

'You should do,' said the man, with a chuckle. 'We worked closely together at the palace before you absconded with Babala.'

'No... no!' cried Fazath, as she slumped to the floor in a faint.

Chapter 5

Babala sobbed as though her heart would break. The smacking stool, over which she was arched, although shaped to take the roundness of her tummy, was hardwood and cupped her mound as if in a clamp. The hands that smacked her bare bottom were as hard as tanned leather, and the blows came rapid and heavy.

Her buttocks were unbearably tender from the blows and the skin glowed, she knew, as if on fire, but for the first time since the Lady Fazath had taken her from the palace she had been provided with an item of clothing. It was skimpy, it was true - a mere square of rough cloth that scarcely covered her sex pouch and swayed enticingly from side to side when she walked.

The smacking stool was positioned beside the great kitchen range, which was filled with burning logs. The other kitchen maids had told her that there was to be one of the Slavemaster's regular banquets that night, and there was much to do. That was earlier in the day, before Babala refused one of the cooks her body, before she was punished upon the smacking stool.

The heat from the fire was as great as the heat in her buttocks and perspiration ran in rivulets between her breasts which were, because of the position the smacking stool kept her, her bottom raised high, free to quiver as each shuddering blow was delivered.

'I'll teach you not to deny me my rights, my pretty young lady!' said the cook, Rata. 'We're worked so hard in this kitchen that having you girls is one of the only perks. You're supposed to open your legs and lift your cunny whenever we need it, which is often in this heat. Didn't the Slavemaster tell you that?'

'I think so,' Babala murmured meekly between sobs.

'Don't give me that,' he yelled. 'Trying to get out of it with your excuses.' The next blow was heavier still and his middle finger slipped into her cunny hole, which Babala knew was wet with her juices. As always the punishment had excited her to the extent that she was open and her clitty stiffly erect. Blushes stained her cheeks with scarlet and she licked her lips nervously, wondering if the cook noticed.

'Excited, eh?' The cook's breathing became noisier and more rapid. So, he *had* noticed! His leathery hand remained still on her beaten bottom, while his thick middle finger slipped deeper into her wetness and the ball of his thumb agitated her nubbin.

'Now why, I wonder,' began Rata, 'since you refused my advances, would you be so excited?'

Babala's sobs receded a little as naughty frissons of pleasure began to swirl in her belly, which was cupped in the smacking stool. 'I do not know, sir,' she answered, untruthfully. 'Truly, I do not know.'

The smacks began again, harder this time, and the fingers drifted deliberately lower to slick between her parted cunny lips. As they reached her flesh pouch they caressed rather than smacked, drawing up fine strings of her juices that coated her castigated buttocks, and the scarlet stains upon Babala's cheeks became deeper as she realised that Rata could feel how very stimulated she was.

'Now will you allow me to fuck you?' he whispered, bending to her ear. He was a handsome man - tall and dark-skinned, his biceps bulging from his sleeveless tunic and his stout thighs strong beneath the short hem. It was very obvious that he was greatly excited by what he had done to Babala. His cock tented his tunic and drove forward under the coarse fabric.

'Yes, sir,' she conceded quietly. 'I should like you to fuck me.' Would the Taskmaster be pleased if he heard her say that, or would he shake his head sorrowfully?

Rata knelt behind her and kissed her flesh folds, allowing his tongue to slip deeply into her cunny, and she could not help but shudder at the sensuous lapping.

'Very hot and juicy,' remarked Rata. 'You wanted me to fuck you all the time.' He gave her a light and playful slap upon her bottom, which even so enhanced the previous beating and Babala could not help but give a little mew of pain.

'But I tease you and there is work to be done,' he continued. 'A great deal of work for the Slavemaster's banquet tonight.'

Babala shuddered as she felt the cook's hardness at her entrance. His globe was thick and it thrust into her in a rush. It opened her fully and her own juices slicked its length to ease its passage. It butted back and forth and her buttocks were slapped by the cook's naked and hirsute belly. The hairs prickled her castigated bottom and increased the soreness caused by the beating. He clearly knew this and seemed to take great delight in rubbing his belly from side to side at the same time as thrusting his cock into her.

Babala could not help the little mews of pain and pleasure, which issued from her full, moist and parted lips. The cook, too, was not entirely silent. He grunted with satisfaction. So noisy were their sounds of sexual activity that other cooks and other maids began to gather round the rutting couple. Not that it was at all unusual for the castle kitchen staff to indulge in copulation over the smacking stool, upon the great pine table, on the floor or against the whitewashed walls, but Babala was a new girl and beautiful at that, with her long golden curls tumbled over her pale shoulders, and the cook had spent a good deal of time upon making her compliant with his wishes.

As the cook drew back for yet another thrust the gathered watchers saw Babala's bottom; saw how blotchy it was from the smacking and how abraded from the grating of the cook's coarse hair.

'A deliciously swollen fleshpot,' commented the pastry cook. 'You've done a fine job there, Rata. She seems to be enjoying it, too. I'll take a turn when you're finished.'

Looking over his broad shoulder and pausing in mid-thrust, Rata, his face flushed with effort and glossed with a fine film of sweat, grinned and gave a brief nod. 'She's a passive girl... amenable when she's been shown the way... juicy and very skilled in clutching a man's tool.' He continued to plunge and Babala closed her eyes in humiliation at the wet noises of their coupling.

At last, Rata gave a final grunt of contentment and she felt him spend into her in several aggressive thrusts. Then she heard the sucking as he pulled from her tightness and she bowed her head in further shame, her cascade of golden hair brushing the filthy floor of the kitchen. She tried to raise herself, but the smacking stool held her tightly, cupped in its hollow.

'Don't move,' said Rata, grinning down at her, as if she had a choice. 'My friend the pastry cook, Marlin, is anxious to try you out.'

'And me!'

'And me!'

'And I'll enjoy giving the little strumpet what she deserves!' This last voice was a woman's, sounding stern and angry. Babala dared to look up from beneath her tumbled hair at the newcomer, and shivered with fright at what she saw.

When the Slavemaster first brought her to the castle he took her into the vast front hall and pointed to a portrait hung at the foot of the great stone staircase. 'My wife,' he said. 'Don't be fooled by her beauty; she is a cruel woman, especially towards someone she suspects might be bedding me.'

The woman was indeed beautiful, thought Babala, looking up at the portrait. She was dark, like the Lady Fazath, with the same fine aristocratic features. Slender, but graciously full at the bosom, she wore her fine clothes well. In the portrait she was dressed in velvet, the bodice of which was encrusted in tiny pearls. The long skirt fell in elegant folds, but at the woman's nipped waist there were several instruments that made Babala shudder. She had looked at the Slavemaster, her sapphire eyes questioning.

'Her little toys,' he'd said with a wry smile. 'No doubt she will demonstrate them to you, given the opportunity. Desilla never misses a chance to use her toys, especially on my new girls, but remember what I said; don't give her an inkling that you and I have coupled.'

Now the woman was here, standing before Babala in the kitchen where she had been so used and humiliated, and where she was held fast on the smacking stool, her bottom raised high and glowing red from its treatment by Rata. Babala tried to close her thighs to hide her sex folds and Rata's copious juices, but the smacking stool was so designed that it would not allow her to hide that part of her body. No matter how she wriggled and squirmed she was held fast by the gripping cup about her tummy.

'Get on with your work,' Desilla ordered, 'or it will be the worse for you... all of you!' The cooks and maids scattered and pretended to be busy with their chopping and kneading of pastry.

Desilla stood over Babala. Shiny black leather boots, thought the girl. She hadn't worn those in the portrait, but dainty pumps such as ladies wore for dancing. Babala raised her head, straining her neck to observe the rest of Desilla's outfit, but was rewarded by a pain that made her arch her back in an attempt to escape the smacking stool's clutches and bite her lip until she tasted blood to mute the scream of agony that rose in her throat.

'Stare at *me*, would you, you little strumpet?' screamed Desilla. 'How *dare* you?'

This time Babala saw the many-stranded lash as it rose through the air. It seemed to move in slow motion and she tensed as she anticipated the pain upon her already tortured bottom. It was worse than anything she had experienced before. It was like cuts with many red-hot knives slicing across the tender flesh of her raised and vulnerable bottom.

'Oh, please madam!' she begged.

'More? You want more?' said Desilla in a husky voice. 'That's good. I like a girl with spirit.'

Babala heard giggles coming from the darkest corners of the kitchen and knew it was the other maids laughing at her distress. 'No, madam,' she managed. 'If it pleases you, madam...'

Desilla knelt before her and Babala could see more clearly what the woman wore. It was a very fine black leather tunic; short, reaching only to the very top of her shapely thighs. The boots were long and the cuffs chafed the woman's full pussy lips at every movement. These, the cunny lips, were darkly bushed like the Lady Fazath's, but where her thighs met them the skin was cleanly shaven, seeming to make the cunny lips stand out more prominently.

'Well, girl,' Desilla said huskily. 'Do you like what you see? For you will be seeing it very intimately in a moment or two.'

The kitchen maids working in the shadows giggled again, but Babala blushed and hung her head. She had not meant to stare at Desilla's cunny. It was just that she could hardly help it with the woman crouching so close and almost thrusting it into her face.

'I think those pretty lips of yours will fit very nicely about my cunt; will do delicious things between my open thighs, but for the time being you can remain clutched in the smacking stool.' She looked about the kitchen and frowned. 'Rata, come here! You've had your fun with this girl and now you can do something for me.'

'Yes, mistress.' Rata was almost grovelling as he hurried over to do the mistress's bidding. 'How may I serve you? Perhaps give the girl another taste of your splendid lash?'

'You can leave that to me,' said Desilla, her words shrill with suppressed anger. 'Bring me a cushion so I do not have to sit upon this filthy and cold floor while the girl services me.'

'Indeed, mistress, at once.'

'And make sure it is made of something soft... velvet or cool satin,' Desilla called as Rata hurried away.

'When you have serviced me to my satisfaction I have all manner of treats for you, my dear,' the woman continued, turning her attention back to Babala, her voice dripping honey. 'What do you say to that?'

'I am very grateful, madam,' the girl said humbly.

'And so you should be.' A shadow appeared by their side; Rata, head bowed in submission and a black satin pillow held out in front of him.

'Idiot!' screamed Desilla. 'If I had wanted black I would have given you strict orders for black, would I not?'

Rata looked cowed. 'I-I suppose you would, madam,' he agreed, in a quavering voice.

Desilla rose to her feet, her strong legs parted to steady her, and lashed out at Rata with her whip, striking him on his broad shoulders. At least, thought Babala ruefully, he wore a tunic to save the full smart of the blow, whereas her bottom caught the full wrath of the wicked instrument.

'Bring me something pretty, something which will show off my cunt to the full as this girl services it with her tongue.' Desilla dismissed him with a wave of her hand and bent to crouch before Babala once more. She wagged a warning finger at her young charge.

'I want this done diligently, young miss,' she said. 'You understand that, don't you?'

'Oh yes, mistress,' said Babala. Hadn't she received the same instructions from the Lady Fazath those long days ago in the forest before the guards caught them?

'Gentle caresses with your tongue and lips,' Desilla went on, 'and you must not mind if the cooks and maids gather round. I enjoy an audience when my cunny is being serviced. It makes it more exciting, you understand?'

'Yes, mistress,' answered Babala, already shaking in the clutches of the smacking stool at the task ahead of her. She knew that if she did not pet Desilla's cunny to her satisfaction it would be the worse for her; that she would feel the lash on her bottom and shoulders until they were raw.

'Ah, here comes Rata with my cushion,' Desilla gushed delightedly, clapping her hands.

Rata bowed and held out a plump satin cushion the colours of which were like jewels - emerald, sapphires, ruby and topaz. They seemed to shimmer and meld into one until Babala blinked her eyes at the brilliance of them.

'That's better, Rata,' Desilla cooed. 'Now place it on the floor in front of the girl and make sure it is close to her so we are in a position nice and close to each other.'

'Yes, mistress,' said Rata, bowing obsequiously, and Babala caught a glimpse of his cock as he bent in front of her. It was stiff and upright under the short tunic and he grinned at her, surreptitiously rubbing it as he placed the cushion in position before Desilla.

'I saw you, Rata,' the woman warned, as she positioned herself on the cushion. 'But I am prepared to ignore your randy little ways on this occasion, you wretch. Now get on with your work.'

Rata bowed deeply as he walked backwards away from the imperious woman, but grinned wickedly at Babala.

Desilla spread her legs, lifting the short leather tunic to give Babala a full view of her flat and muscular stomach and neatly trimmed bush. 'Can you reach my fleshpot, my dear?' she asked. 'Or shall I move closer?'

Babala looked at the pouting outer sex leaves, which framed a flushed cunny, and knew the woman was intensely excited. 'Just a little nearer,' she said submissively, stroking her tongue around her lips to moisten them for the task ahead.

Desilla lifted her knees and spread them outwards, giving Babala full access to her cunny. She leaned back on her elbows, her eyes heavy with anticipation of the joys to come.

'You may pet my bottom hole, my dear,' said Desilla, as though bestowing a great favour upon Babala, 'but make sure you do this when you have fully serviced my cunt.'

'Yes, mistress,' said Babala.

Tongue generously coated with saliva, Babala touched Desilla's clitty with the very tip and stroked the pouting outer leaves of her flesh pouch.

'Not like that!' Desilla was incensed with fury. She sat up and fumbled for the lash, which she had placed behind her head. 'Stupid girl! What do you think I am - a piece of china that will break at the slightest touch?' The woman arched her arm back and the long strands of the lash beat upon Babala's tortured bottom, making her strain and mew with pain.

'Oh, I am so sorry, madam!' she managed, trying desperately to catch her breath, which seemed to be beaten from her by the lash. 'I shall try to do better!'

'Not try, girl!' Desilla spat. 'Do! Do! Understand?' She was already repositioning herself before Babala, legs spread and knees raised, but she kept the lash loosely clasped in her long fingers, ready to beat the girl given the slightest excuse.

'Yes, madam,' Babala whimpered, swallowing a sob, for she knew that sobs would simply anger Desilla more.

'Now lick me, girl,' ordered the woman, 'tenderly but firmly. Lick my clitty; go deeply into my opening as if your tongue was a little cock, stiff and thrusting. Do you think you can do that?' This last was said as if Desilla was speaking to someone lacking in normal intelligence.

'Yes, madam,' whispered Babala, her voice quivering with trepidation. She raised her head to look at the woman. More than handsome, she was almost beautiful with her raven hair and her dark eyes gleaming with pent-up lust. Her lips were full and red, although this was natural rather than painted with carmine, as some aristocratic women were wont to do in Brentasi. They curved and parted in a sensual smile as her free hand entangled itself in Babala's hair, urging her to bury her pretty face into the openness of her cunt.

The woman's musk was strong, but not unpleasant. Babala licked the underside of her clitty stem, which was long and engorged. She heard Desilla moan in ecstasy and transferred her petting to the tip, which was bared and the hood drawn back. At the same time she thrust a trembling middle finger into the woman's pulsing cunny.

'Two fingers, my precious,' Desilla instructed, 'or even three, but do not make me come too soon. Make my pleasure last, or...' she thrashed the stone floor with the whip, making Babala start and lose the rhythm of her licking. Instantly the tips of the leather strands swept down upon her bottom, making her mew into the liquid softness of Desilla's cunt.

With trembling fingers Babala thrust into the soft and welcoming cunny, and felt those fingers clutched by the woman's muscular fleshpot.

'Hm, that feels delicious, my darling,' murmured Desilla. 'Just slow down the licking, but make sure you lap from the base of my stem to the very tip. No quick side-to-side little smacks with that lovely tongue of yours.'

Desilla began to shudder and Babala knew she was very close to her orgasm. Her cunny was saturated with juices that glazed Babala's cheeks and chin.

'Slow down,' Desilla said hoarsely. 'You must slow down. I do not wish you to make me come so soon. Stop it this instant...' The whip lashed Babala's shoulders but the blow was weak, without strength, and was a mere tickle compared to those that went before.

Babala stopped her petting and stroked Desilla's smooth buttocks in an almost tender fashion. The woman's breathing slowed, but Babala became aware of the audience that had gathered and the murmurs that grew in volume as the moments passed.

'She will have you opening her rear hole before you know it,' said Rata.

'Yes!' exclaimed a girl, pretty as a picture and no older than Babala. 'That's what she did to me, but she tires of the new girls very quickly.'

Babala felt her cheeks flush and burn scarlet that she should be placed in such a humiliating position.

'How dare you talk of me in such a fashion?!' Desilla lashed about the watchers with her whip and they staggered back, holding their hurts and cringing at their owner's anger. 'I am mistress of this castle and I own every one of you!'

The watchers scuttled away to their duties and Desilla and Babala were again alone.

'Lick me again, my sweet,' ordered Desilla. 'But this time as I begin my orgasm touch your tongue to my rear hole, but then touch the pulsing little rose with your finger until it is drawn in by my convulsing.'

Babala could not help wondering how she would know these exact moments; how she would know when to lick and when to finger. 'How...? she began, a curious frown on her flushed face.

'Oh, come now,' Desilla's face wore a wry and sarcastic smirk. 'Come now, don't pretend that you have no knowledge of such matters. My husband, the Slavemaster, gave me to understand that you are well-versed in such matters.' She lay back, resting on one elbow and stroking her open flesh pouch with the soft strands of the whip. 'What was the word he used?' She made a pretence at frowning. 'Used? Yes, that was it... *used*. Fit for nothing except a whore house or this kitchen where the cooks can use you as they wish.'

Babala bowed her head to hide the spots of scarlet that blossomed on her cheeks. How could she help it if the guards used her day after torturous day? She had been too weak to defend herself and the Lady Fazath was bonded to the cave wall. 'I did not intend to - '

'But you did, didn't you?' Desilla mocked, waving the whip that now smelled so strongly of her musk. 'But we waste time. You know what I want of you and I want it now.'

Once again Babala began to lick, her petting firm, just as Desilla desired. The fingering, too, seemed to please the mistress of the castle for she groaned and shuddered, pressed her cunny closer and closer to Babala's smeared mouth.

'Yes!' gasped Desilla. 'I am very close now. You may pet my bottom hole, but very gently. Let my climax last for... let it last for *eons*.'

Babala felt a sob rise in her throat and tears wet her cheeks. How could anyone make an orgasm last forever? For eons? And if she did not please the mistress what terrible punishment would she receive?

The bottom hole was tight and Babala's tongue could feel the tiny pleats gathered at the minute hole. She caressed it, pushing two fingers into the pulsing cunny at the same time. These became coated with a slick cream that slithered over the heel of her hand. Her tongue-tip slipped into her mistress's rose-hole and she felt the woman arch in pleasure. She moaned, and the moan became a wail.

'A finger in there, you stupid girl. Don't you listen to my instructions?' Desilla was thrashing her lower body from side to side upon the cushion and Babala was hard pressed to finger the rose-hole or the pulsing and dripping cunny, but she managed it although her hands were trembling uncontrollably.

At last it was over and Desilla lay back upon the cushion, the colours of which were darkened with her sap. 'Not the best of petting,' grumbled the woman. Babala drooped her head, hiding her tearstained face and the soft lips which were sticky with her mistress's juices, fearing the sting of the lash upon her bottom, still sore from Rata's heavy hand and the quickness of Desilla's whip. 'But not the worst, either. I think you could be trained to please me greatly. Would you like that?'

Babala was at a loss to answer. She was a slave, taken from the auction by the Slavemaster and of little worth at that. She had no choice but to agree.

'Yes, mistress,' she said meekly, in a subdued manner.

'You don't sound entirely convincing.' Desilla was stern and Babala watched her fingers twitch about the handle of the lash.

'I am trained, madam.' Babala's voice trembled as she spoke. Perhaps those words would have been better left unsaid.

Desilla frowned and straightened the short skirt of her black leather tunic. 'But only by a whoremaster, surely?' Her handsome features were distorted in a supercilious smile.

'No, mistress,' said Babala, trying to ease the aches in her cramped body, which was so tightly held in the clutches of the smacking stool.

'Who then?' Desilla's dark eyes became slits and her full lips became thin and pursed. 'The guards?' She threw back her head and let out a mirthless laugh.

'The Taskmaster,' admitted Babala. 'He trained me beautifully at the palace of Ellipsis.' The very thought of the Taskmaster's expertise made naughty little frissons of delight quiver through her tortured body, but at the same time tears of longing for her old life filled her sapphire eyes and tumbled down her pale cheeks like liquid pearls.

Chapter 6

Sharp slaps brought the Lady Fazath to her senses, but as her consciousness returned she screamed and a large hand cupped her mouth, muting her cries.

'Be quiet, you fool!' hissed a deep voice. 'Do you want the whole forest, the whole of Brentasi to know we're here?' He loosened his grip upon her mouth and chin, but immediately he did so she screamed once more.

'I didn't want to do this,' said the man, 'but needs must when the devil drives.' With two long strides he reached the other side of the tiny cottage and took a bullwhip from a hook on the rough stone wall. 'You asked for it... in fact, you have been asking for it these many days. How dare you take Babala from the palace? How dare you? All my weeks of training to make her a pliant girl were for nothing, and she was for the Prince, not you.'

The whip snaked over his huge shoulders and thrashed down upon her, cutting a swathe of scarlet across the tawny skin of her naked back.

'Oh, Taskmaster!' moaned the Lady Fazath, for with the disguise thrown off it was clearly him. 'I had to have her! She is so beautiful, so sensual, and so very feminine. Don't you understand? She was the sort of girl a woman like me could not resist.' The Lady Fazath looked repentant although still proud and upright. 'I am sorry, Taskmaster.'

The bull whip cut through the air once more and the sound of its thrashing echoed against the walls of the cottage so many times that it seemed there were a hundred whips flying through the small space.

'You will be, my lady,' hissed the Taskmaster. 'I promise you that. If I was to take you to Ellipsis this moment and hand you to the Prince...'

He stood over her, so large and powerful, so virile in his jewelled loincloth, and Fazath knelt at his feet, clutching him around the calves in a most uncharacteristic manner.

'Please, no! He will execute me. My head will fall. Surely after all we have been to each other - such close friends - you would not do that to me?' Her heavy breasts brushed against the roughness of his hairy legs and she felt her nipples become painfully stiff. She was surprised at her own sudden submissiveness.

'It is what you deserve!' he snapped, but he pulled her to her feet and drew the handle of the folded bullwhip beneath her bare breasts. She shuddered but did not protest; dared not, even when one of his large hands cupped the toned firmness of a breast. 'I always found you desirable, Fazath,' he said, and he spoke softly, almost lovingly.

'But I do not...'

'I know - it's always been the girls that attract you.' He looked into her eyes and the smouldering lust in his made her shudder in his arms. She could feel the strength of his need beneath his loincloth. It was stiff and thick, pulsing, and she felt the end globe, bared of its hood and damp with pre-issue against her belly. For the briefest of moments Fazath felt a yearning, which made her legs lose their strength and her belly become heavy as if a great weight was suddenly dropped within it. Her cunny felt heavy and she felt moisture and heat, a sudden opening of her folds and a thrill in her clitty.

'Stop this,' she said, pulling away from him. 'You know my tastes. You know why I took Babala. Didn't you hear me; hear me tell you that she became an obsession with me?'

'Because she was the most beautiful girl in the Prince's harem.' The Taskmaster pulled her to him once more and there was no possibility of escape so great was the strength of his grip. 'But tell me, Fazath,' he said, an ironic smile twisting his handsome features, 'which would you rather endure?' He stroked the edge of his thumb down the contour of her cheek and jawbone, smiling into her eyes all the time. 'Execution, or my cock?'

The Lady Fazath gasped and again tried to escape the iron strength of his grip. She could not speak for several seconds. Her tongue clove to the roof of her mouth and felt dry as dust, but at last she regained the power of speech. 'I have no choice.' She looked at him steadily, her dark eyes narrowed and her lips thinned in distaste.

'No, you have no choice, Fazath,' said the Taskmaster, 'but you endured the guards, so surely you would not find me too much of a trial?' He looked almost sad as he said this, his eyes shone with moisture, but the expression was gone in a flash and his lips hardened in a tense smile. 'Will you?' he added.

'I suppose not,' admitted Fazath. 'How would you like me? Bound and resentful or free and submissive?'

'I want you resentful, Fazath,' he told her, 'so that when it is all over you will be so grateful that you will do exactly as I wish.'

The Lady Fazath shrugged. 'What will you bind me with? Ropes, manacles? I have endured all of that with the guards. Nothing could be worse than what they did to me.'

'Really? I have a chair here, which will imprison you as you have never been imprisoned before. Once you were dominant and lording it over the girls in the harem...' His hand traced the swell of her breasts, the dip of her waist, the neat mound of her belly and once more Fazath felt the wicked thrill of desire surge through her. 'Now what are you?'

'Your slave, Taskmaster,' she said, in a voice she did not recognise as her own.

'Yes, bought and paid for.' His words were punctuated with a chuckle. 'Let me show you this chair.' He took her hand and led her to a shadowy corner of the room, and there stood a tall chair, reached by two steps. There were straps on the arms to hold her wrists, and at the base to hold her ankles wide apart.

Standing up from the seat of the chair was a large phallus constructed of hardened black leather; causing her terrible consternation, and she turned to question the Taskmaster.

He threw back his head and laughed. 'I shall not leave any orifice of yours un-stimulated, my dear. I shall do things to you I would not have dreamed of doing to your girls. You will beg for mercy. Your orgasms will come thick and fast and there will be pain, my dear. Oh, yes! There will be a great deal of pain, but this will only enhance your joy.' Again he held her to him, her upper arms clamped in his vice-like grip, and his mouth raped hers in a kiss that left her breathless and weak. 'I have longed to do that for years, Fazath, but you were so untouchable I did not dare.'

Anger gave her the strength to release one arm from his hold and her hand swiped his face in a resounding slap, jerking his head to one side.

'You will pay for that, Fazath,' he said slowly, glowering at her. 'Believe me, you will pay.'

His strength made her own seem puny and he pushed her roughly to the chair. With swift and decisive movements he strapped her ankles to the wide apart wooden legs, leaving her sex vulnerable, the black leather phallus standing lewdly between her thighs, brushing her cunny but not entering it.

'What torture is this, Taskmaster?' Fazath was scathing, her lips twisted in an ironic smile. 'The phallus does not enter me, but its stalk merely kisses the very tip of my clitty.'

'Be patient, my love,' he said as he tightened the leather straps at her wrists, and Fazath winced as the leather cut into the tawny skin of her arms. 'I have always loved the secretiveness of a bottom in a handsome woman,' he said. The chair was designed in such a fashion as to push her buttocks forward and open the cheeks to fully display Fazath's secret hole, and the Taskmaster ran his thumb across the wrinkled tightness, which flexed involuntarily. He chuckled. 'There is something very forbidden about a woman's bottom hole. I was always careful to resist Babala's; to leave it for the Prince should he wish to breach it, but because of your stupidity it was well used by the guards. I am determined to make you pay dearly for that indiscretion.'

With many questions in her dark eyes Fazath watched as he smeared the black leather phallus with a sweet-scented balm. It made the leather shine and gleam in the candlelit gloom.

'Raise yourself up in the straps,' ordered the Taskmaster.

'But I'm too tightly bound,' Fazath objected.

'No, no; you will find there is just sufficient leeway for you to lift your bottom.'

The straps cut more tightly into her skin as she strained against them to lift herself, and felt the Taskmaster adjusting the angle of the phallus so that the bulbous tip was positioned exactly at her rear opening. There was a slight pressure as the globe pressed open the tight pleats, and then an increasing fullness as the black leather length pushed into the tightness. Fazath moaned, not from the pain, but from the pleasurable sensation as her clitty and sex were stimulated from within.

The Taskmaster gently rubbed three fingertips around the open moistness of her cunny. He massaged her nubbin with her own juices, and with the pressure from within and the gentle stimulation on the outside she felt her legs become weak and heavy in the bonds.

The Taskmaster laughed. 'Oh, I have not finished yet, my love. I want total submission from you, and to get that I know I must go much further.'

Red-hot pain shot from Fazath's nipples as toothed clips were fastened upon the tightly erect buds. She groaned and tried to slump deeper in the chair, but the wrist straps and the phallus plunging deeper into her bottom held her fast.

'I have more of these,' he said, rattling a metal container before her eyes. 'I have always found the toothed clips a great help in subduing reluctant girls.'

'I'm not a girl!' managed Fazath. 'I'm a woman.'

'But one who will be a great deal more womanly if taught to be submissive.'

'Oh, be *quiet*...' Frissons of bliss shot through her body, making her taut and muscular belly ripple. She felt pearly dewdrops gather on her sex lips and more juices trickle down between her buttocks, and froze as a neat string of tiny clips were attached to her inner folds, fastening them to the plump outer leaves. He had made her more open than ever.

'This isn't my style,' she gasped. 'You said yourself that I'm dominant.'

'But not when the guards used you,' he rasped. 'Shackled you to the cave wall; did all manner of things to your handsome body.'

The Lady Fazath hung her head, just as she had seen Babala do many times, both at the harem and when captured in the forest. Was the Taskmaster truly making her submissive, as he had threatened to do?

'Beautiful,' he murmured, and she saw him staring at the open flesh of her sex and saw his penis throb beneath his jewelled loincloth. The clips, she knew, made her sex more available, revealed it more clearly.

She gasped as the length of a finger tested her sex, felt the width of her opening. 'Good, Fazath,' he said softly. 'You are becoming womanly. Your cunt is acting as a woman's should. It is ready for a man's cock.'

Fazath's eyes blazed and she pursed her lips, gathering spittle in her mouth, and spat at him. But his only reaction was to laugh heartily.

'I think I can find a better use for those lovely lips,' he said, and she could only watch helplessly as he climbed athletically upon the arms of the chair and pushed the jewelled loincloth to one side to expose the magnificence of his penis. The satiny globe, slick and purple, pulsed with intent before her eyes. She was mesmerized by the oozing pore at its tip, which swiftly stretched her lips apart, slipping deeper and deeper into her throat until she had engulfed the whole length. The taste was less bitter than the spume of the guards, almost wholesome, and she gladly engulfed it until her lips were nestled in the crisp curls of the Taskmaster's pubis.

Fazath's lips slid up and down the thick shaft, caressing it at each slick passage. She could hear him moaning with pleasure and felt him pushing back and forth rhythmically as she petted his sperm sac with her tongue at each full-length massage. She could not believe her own enjoyment in her forced passivity; imprisoned in the chair and being degraded by the man who was her equal at the palace.

With a grunt of satisfaction he pulled from her and climbed from his perch, holding his pulsing girth in both hands, spraying her with jet after jet of creamy come. She arched her neck back, surprising herself yet again as she welcomed the splashes of spillage. One hung like a pearl upon her lower lip and she licked it, tasting with enjoyment, but the moment passed and she looked at him with hatred in her eyes.

'Still not subdued, Fazath?' he asked, putting his length to rights and tucking it behind the square of jewelled cloth. 'Still determined to be a man rather than a woman?'

'Let me out of this thing,' she cursed, straining at the leather bindings and against the phallus that was plugged so firmly in her rear hole, 'and I'll show you how I fight as well as any man...'

The Taskmaster smiled, but said nothing. He crouched down and Fazath stiffened, straining against the wrist straps and trying to close her legs, but the ankle straps kept them wide apart. With a feather-light touch he stroked her inner thighs until she thought she would scream with the gentle titillation. He smiled up at her as his thumbs drew nearer and nearer her spread sex pouch.

Lithe as an animal, his cock stiff once more behind the loincloth, he sniffed her musk. 'You are beginning to smell like a woman, Fazath,' he said in a voice husky with lust.

She tried to move, tried to hide her sex, but it was useless. Each movement merely served to push the leather phallus deeper into her bottom, push forward her clitty and open her up more fully.

'Don't you like being a woman?' he asked in a teasing manner. He kissed the tip of her clitty and she could not help but whisper a long sigh of pleasure. 'Don't you, Fazath?'

'Of course I do,' she whispered breathily. 'But you know what I am; what I like.'

'I'm beginning to wonder.' He kissed her again, this time closing his lips around her throbbing clitty and allowing his tongue to lap back and forth against its root. Fazath tried to butt against his caresses, urging him to do more, but her open flesh muffled a deep-throated chuckle. She felt a finger thrust into her, heard the noise of her juices against the intrusion. The finger drew back and forth and, despite what she had so recently told the Taskmaster, Fazath felt a fever of excitement at her own nakedness, her helplessness, her open vulnerability.

'Your flesh seeps, Fazath,' he said, and drawing back he held up the finger he'd pushed into her. It was coated heavily with her dew, slick and shimmering in the candlelit gloom, with trails of pearly cream following one after the other down the finger to its base.

He touched the tip of the digit to her lips. She could smell her own musk, heavy and wanton, and her nostrils flared at the scent of it.

A knowing smile lit his handsome features. 'You delight in the smell of a woman.'

'I've made no secret of it.'

'And the taste?' He forced open her lips and thrust the finger deeper. At the same time he petted her spread sex lips, the scarlet jutting bud which lay in its centre and the black tip of leather that protruded from her bottom.

Fazath sucked greedily on the finger, sighing; how she yearned for the sweet taste of a woman!

Suddenly the stifling air in the little cottage was cut by the swish of a whip. The long length of supple leather caught Fazath beneath the breasts while the tip of it caressed one of her nipples, twitching the silver clip that held it fast. A faint mew of surprise escaped her lips as the finger was removed from her mouth. Her dark eyes widened and then flashed angrily.

'I wasn't aware I'd done anything to displease you,' she said. 'Wasn't I being womanly? Wasn't I being submissive?'

'You were enjoying your own taste.' The whip beat the air again, flicked her body and lashed her belly, which pouted because of the leather phallus pushing from within.

'Is that not allowed?' Fazath's dark eyes were not cowed, but defiant even when the whip made her body arch with the force of the third blow.

'I want you womanly, as a female should be to a man.' He stood over her, muscular legs astride, the loincloth tented by the fullness of his cock and the whip raised to give her another blow. 'I want you to see my cock as something magnificent, something to be revered.' He pulled the jewelled cloth to the side to give her full sight of it spearing upwards from his dark pubic bush, with his full and heavy balls slightly drawn up between his tanned thighs.

'Then you will wait forever,' she vowed, her wide lips curved in a sneering smile. 'I can never do that.'

'You may regret that one day,' he warned, and his voice was menacing. He flung the whip into a corner and stood with his back to her, busy with something upon a crude shelf, and she had to admit that his rear view was attractive. His buttocks were taut, bare and clothed only by the thong of leather that spanned his waist to hold the loincloth in place.

'What are you doing?' she felt compelled to ask.

'All in good time,' he said, she heard the clink of metal, and the sound was sinister and made her shudder.

'What little toy are you going to tease me with this time?' She knew there was a sneer in her voice and she was probably heaping more pain and discomfort upon herself, but she could not help it.

'This is no toy, believe me, my dear.'

'Oh, the suspense is killing me.' Fazath, for all her helplessness in the chair, the pain at her wrists and ankles, her vulnerable and open sex, could not help taunting her former colleague.

'It will not kill you,' said the Taskmaster, turning to face her, his hands lovingly clasped about an iron object, 'but it will keep you quiet.'

Fazath cringed as he approached her. It looked like a helmet, but it was far more intricate than merely that.

'The scold's bridle, Fazath,' he said, standing over her. 'You've probably heard of it.'

'But I'm not a scold!' Fazath strained against the leather restraints.

'That's for me to decide.'

Fazath felt the cold hardness of the metal against her scalp, even through the lustrous thickness of her black hair. She thrashed her head back and forth in a vain attempt to escape the bridle, but he was too strong for her and the lower part of the wicked helmet slid down over her forehead.

'No need to worry, my dear,' said the Taskmaster, in a tone that made her distinctly uneasy. 'You will be able to breathe and see...'

'But not speak!' finished Fazath.

'Quite right.' The helmet slid further and she could feel the chill of the iron against her cheeks, her mouth. He fastened straps beneath her chin so that her head was imprisoned, as was her body. 'And finally...'

She tasted iron on her tongue as a plug of metal was pressed down upon it, and iron also pressed tightly about her lips and cheeks. Her face was kept entirely immobile.

'There is just one drawback with this charming little device,' he said, admiring his handiwork. 'I cannot use your delightful lips to caress my cock, but then...' He began to release the tiny clips that held her sex.

Dearly would Fazath have delighted to sigh with relief, but the bridle kept her tongue still within her mouth. Her sex lips remained fully open and her nubbin was hard and erect in the moist bed of her pouch.

'Can you guess what I am going to do now, Fazath?' She shook her head, her eyes wide behind the mask. The clips were removed from her nipples, a fingernail flicked each and shots of pain speared through the full taut mounds. 'This...' He pulled the loincloth to one side and revealed his stiffness. 'This again needs some relief, and since I have locked up your mouth, what else can I do but use you as a woman should be used?'

It would do her no good to struggle - Fazath knew that. Her wrists and ankles were already chafed by the tightness of the leather restraints. The iron lever clamped her tongue. She could not even scream, but did she wish to do so?

Dark eyes riveted to his upright shaft, she felt her inner lips quiver. She could feel her cunny open and inviting. Her sap seeped over her bottom cheeks, wetting the leather that was still firmly inserted within her rear hole.

Lithely, he climbed upon the chair again and slid his legs about her waist. She could feel his globe caressing her slick entrance, petting her clitty, which throbbed eagerly. Why did she feel like this? She was almost willing! Was it really because he had made her helpless and vulnerable?

He rubbed his cock tip up and down her wet slit. 'Is this not much nicer than the dildo you use upon yourself and the girls in the harem?' He played the thick length up and down her slippery opening, never once dipping into her cunny.

Fazath remained very still. If she was to tell the truth, the touch of his organ on her sex flesh was stimulating. She would have liked to urge him into her, but it went against her grain since he had gone to such lengths to make her helpless to do this deed. Her arms ached intolerably, imprisoned by the straps. Her legs too, stretched open for such a long period, pained her beyond bearing. Her tongue captured by the lever was dry and she tasted the cold metal, but still she bore it without protest. It was so unlike her. What had he done to her - to her mind as well as her body?

With his thumbs he spread her sex lips, which were still tender from the spreading open with the clips. He dabbed his thick globe at her opening and, had she been able, Fazath would have gasped at the sensation. It was so smooth, so turgid. The feeling was quite different to the dildo she had so often used upon herself. It was hard, thick, living flesh that, as he pressed forward into her seemed to meld with her own. She wanted to arch up towards his thrust, but she was held fast by the leather bonds. If she could only scream her needs, but this, too, was denied her.

'Are you enjoying it, Fazath?' he asked, pressing her open as he pushed forward.

She could feel the heated throb in her clitty as it was chafed by his turgid girth; could feel the glorious sensation of liquidity in her lower belly. In her female opening there was a sensation that she had never felt before - the beginnings of a climax.

'You are, aren't you?' The Taskmaster was almost fully embedded in her now and she could feel the rub of his lush pubic bush rasping against hers. She tried to shake her head, to deny her pleasure, but he grasped the long cascade of black hair that escaped from the iron bridle, arching the pale length of her throat and thrusting the fullness of her breasts upwards. Still impaled within her he lowered his head and took the pliant flesh of her breast within his mouth, sucking and biting.

'Don't deny the pleasure I'm giving you,' he said, lifting his head. He tugged harder on her hair, arching her body further, thrusting fully into her. Behind the mask her lips were forced open, bonded by the iron, but she knew he wanted to kiss her, to ravage her mouth, cruelly and yet tenderly. It was a strange knowledge.

She also knew her orgasm was close. Pleasure seemed to radiate from his cock, from her clitoris, from her pulsing cunny.

'It will be very soon now,' he grunted. 'My come will fountain into you. I will possess you at last, Fazath. You will be truly my slave and you will do my bidding for the rest of our lives together.'

A heaviness, a weakness came over her as her cunny petted his thrusting cock. Was this what she wanted after all?

He gave a triumphant cry and she felt him stiffen, and her own pleasure sent her soaring high above the chair where she had been bonded for so long. Vaguely, she felt her cushiony walls suck upon his thickness, draining every drop of his manly fluid into her depths.

Chapter 7

Desilla was leaving the kitchen. Her hard but beautiful face was distorted by a frown. Looking over her shoulder she stared at Babala, her eyes questioning and her mouth drawn into a cold hard line.

'Take her from the smacking stool and chain her,' she said. 'There is something about that girl I don't trust.' Babala shuddered at her tone and was aware of a quake of fear in her belly as Desilla gave her another penetrating look and spoke again. 'Chain her securely and then bring her to me.'

Babala felt herself trembling from head to foot with fear. She remembered how the Slavemaster had warned her to keep silent about what they had done in the carriage. But surely that was not her fault? She was his slave and as such must obey him. She had said nothing; nothing that could possibly give the woman any inkling of the intimacy that took place between her and the woman's husband.

With some difficulty she was lifted from the smacking stool, her belly tender from where the device had clasped her for so long. She stood on legs that would barely support her, and the toned flesh trembled.

Rata stood before her. 'You're in trouble now, young miss.'

'But I've done nothing wrong,' protested Babala. That was not quite true, she admitted to herself, but there was nothing that Desilla could know.

'You are young and beautiful,' said Rata. 'That's the problem.' He touched her breasts. 'These have the perfect roundness of youth and yet...' he hefted each mound in turn, feeling the lower swells. 'And yet they are heavy with maturity. A delightful combination.'

Babala felt a flush of embarrassment stain her cheeks at the compliment.

'And this...' Rata touched the tender swell of her belly. 'Rounded and yet not overly so, and such a neat little navel.' He pushed the square of cloth that was Babala's only item of clothing to one side and dipped a fingertip into the pleasing little hollow, before trailing it down to the triangle of golden curls. 'And this nest is perfection.'

Again Babala felt a flush of heat stain her cheeks and she lowered her head, but this only made her predicament worse for she could see his hands stroking the place where her thighs met her pubis, caressing the delicate flesh.

'It pouts so prettily and the golden curls upon it do not hide the lovely darkness within.' A rough fingertip slipped into the valley between the plump lips and Babala could not help but arch against the intrusion. 'All this beauty is the problem, you see,' explained Rata, and Babala frowned, silently questioning him. 'Desilla is envious of your youth and beauty,' he went on. 'She thinks you will steal Maxim - the Slavemaster, her husband - from her.'

'But that's silly,' protested Babala. 'I'm nothing but a slave, and a used one at that. She has nothing to fear from me. Nothing.' She lowered her head once more and her golden curls curtained her face. 'What can she possibly fear from me?'

Rata shrugged. 'Who knows what goes on in Desilla's mind?' His rough hands caressed the contours of her body, the swell of her breasts and the sharp dip of her waist and the curve of her hips. His touch made Babala tremble for it was delightfully sensual for all its roughness. 'But I have to obey her orders.'

'I know,' Babala said sadly, looking at the light chains Rata dangled from one hand and which had, only moments before, tickled the parts he now touched. 'We'd best do it, Rata, or you will be in trouble too.'

He bent to kiss her softly on the lips and smiled before he began his task, and her hands were quickly shackled together with iron manacles.

'Is it uncomfortable?' he asked.

'A little,' said Babala. 'Only a little.'

'Try to relax the muscles,' he advised. 'You are a brave girl, Babala. I know you will stand what befalls you with fortitude.'

Manacles gripped her ankles and these were held at full stretch by a further bar keeping her legs held wide apart. 'How am I supposed to walk?' she asked timorously.

'Oh, don't worry about that,' said Rata. 'I shall carry you in a cart.'

Babala was shocked. 'Through the castle?'

'Of course - you'd hardly expect to be taken around the crag. I am sure Desilla would not be so unfeeling as to have me tip you over the mountainside.'

Babala shuddered, but the slight movement made her limbs ache yet more. 'But everyone will stare,' she protested, shyly looking up at Rata.

'And no doubt want to touch you here...' he rolled his palms over her taut nipples and then kissed them. 'And certainly here...' he pushed aside the scrap of cloth behind which was hidden Babala's pert mound, and cupped the fullness. 'And here...' he parted her full sex lips to reveal the flushed nubbin, which lay in the succulent bed. In her chained helplessness Babala could do nothing to hide her vulnerability. She could only allow Rata to do as he pleased, and she knew there would be many others who would take advantage of her predicament - courtiers and servants alike. She bent her head in sad submission, but almost immediately Rata forced her chin up and made her look at him.

'If they see you weeping and playing the sad little maid,' he warned, 'they will only taunt you more. Be brave, that's my advice.'

'I'll try,' said Babala as he lifted her in his arms.

The cart was crudely made and sloped down so that she was displayed as Rata trundled her through the dark passages that led from the kitchens. As they came to the more luxuriously appointed parts of the castle Babala blinked at the brightness. Sconces flared from the walls and chandeliers holding hundreds of candles hung from the high ceilings. There was no point in hoping that she could hide in shadowy corners.

'Now, what have we here?'

Babala closed her eyes as if by doing so she could hide her nakedness and those parts of her that were so clearly revealed by the positioning of the chains which held her.

'The new girl,' said Rata, halting the cart. 'I have orders to take her to Desilla's quarters.'

The man who had stopped them, a courtier, raised his eyebrows. 'Then I had better make the most of this beauty. There are some who say that girls who are taken there never come out again.'

Babala shuddered, wished she was clothed more fully and was less tightly chained. If only she could somehow escape.

Reacting to an unspoken command Rata obediently tipped the cart up and back so that the courtier had less far to bend and Babala's cunny was at a convenient level for him to inspect.

The courtier pushed the square of cloth to the side with a gold-headed walking stick, which he used more for show than to help any infirmity. The gold knob was stroked across Babala's sex curls, the richly dressed gentleman clearly enjoying her helplessness and vulnerability.

At the thought of being displayed in this public place Babala felt her juices begin to flow. She struggled against such a wanton reaction, but it was useless. Her arms and legs were held immobile by the chains and bars. If only the courtier knew that her sap flowed because she was trained to please! Tears fell unchecked from her lashes, spilling down her cheeks and onto the upper slopes of her breasts, glistening like morning dew.

The courtier, about to open Babala's sex lips with the gold head of his walking cane, looked puzzled. 'Why does she weep?' he asked of nobody in particular. 'Is she shy? Is she a virgin?' His eyes glinted with excitement at this latter thought. The gold knob, as bulbous and perfectly round as a man's cock globe, hesitated between her plump sex lips.

'Sadly, sir,' said Rata, shaking his head, 'no, she is not a virgin. Maxim obtained her for free because she was so used, but Desilla seems to have taken her for herself.'

Shrugging, the courtier pressed open Babala's sex folds, rather eccentrically pushing them from side to side to peer within. 'Ah, now,' he murmured, to himself again, 'she is a truly delicious morsel.'

'Indeed she is, sir,' agreed Rata, moving round to the front of the cart to ogle Babala's open sex lips as though he had not seen them before. He rubbed his crotch beneath his tunic as his cock stiffened and tented the short garment.

'Have you had the girl?' The courtier pressed the gold knob deeper between the folds until Babala felt it caress the hard fullness of her nubbin.

Rata looked shamefaced and hung his head.

'Have you?' persisted the courtier. Others joined the small group standing by the cart, courtiers and servants alike.

'Yes, sir,' admitted Rata, after some hesitation. 'She is easy and eager for men to take her, especially in the heat of the kitchens.'

Babala's tears fell faster. That was so unfair! She had no choice but to allow Rata to take her. Why was he being so cruel?

The crowd around the cart murmured excitedly and pushed closer to her. The gold knob was thrust deeper into the soft moistness of her cunny and she gasped as she felt it butt the limits of her womb.

The murmurs grew in volume. 'Thrust it in and out!' someone urged from the back of the crowd. 'Let's see her come.'

'Oh, yes!' enthused a woman. Babala heard hands being clapped gleefully, and no matter how she tried to stem her tears she could not and they fell like pearls, splashing the smooth swells of her breasts. Rata seemed to be enjoying the humiliation she was suffering, and she had been beginning to consider him an ally.

The cane was thrust rapidly in and out of her cunny and Babala could not help but clutch the hard and unyielding rod. She knew her juices flowed heavily and would glisten upon the dark wood. Her clitty jerked spasmodically at each rub of it. She knew her orgasm was close and there was nothing she could do to prevent it. The crowd was silent, waiting with baited breath. Some of the men were openly rubbing their cocks, slicking the smooth skin up and down their stiffened rods. One woman, her mouth open and her tongue lapping about her lips, lifted her skirt and pressed open her pussy lips to rub at her clitty with obvious relish.

'She is nothing but a whore,' said the courtier who had first stopped by the cart. 'She shows such great pleasure in having objects thrust into her cunt, she can be nothing more than that.'

Despite the cruel words Babala could not help the waves of pleasure as her climax took her over. The watching eyes of the crowd, the courtier and Rata, meant nothing to her; for those few moments nothing mattered but the ecstasy of her orgasm.

'And what, may I ask, is going on here?'

Desilla's voice broke the silence and all eyes looked in her direction. She was dressed in a tightly laced corset that whittled her waist to unbelievably tiny dimensions. It was fashioned from black leather, shiny and supple. It reached the tops of her thighs, leaving her sex bush bare, which Babala could see she had taken great pains to have her maid groom to perfection.

Her boots were fashioned from the same lustrous black leather. The toes were pointed and the heels high and spiked. Unlike the boots she had worn in the kitchen, these only reached her calves, where they fitted snugly. From the lower margin of the corset hung several objects, the use of which Babala was sure she would experience very shortly.

'Did I not tell you to bring that girl to my chambers?' Desilla demanded of Rata. '*Immediately*.'

'I was doing so,' he said nervously, 'but the sire here showed great interest in her and wished to be shown her attributes.'

Desilla snatched the gold knob from Babala's cunny and viciously thrashed everyone about her with the rod. 'This girl is my slave! Do you understand?'

The courtier cowered under Desilla's onslaught and begged forgiveness. 'The girl has such beckoning eyes, simply asking to be satisfied, madam!'

Babala gasped at the lie and tried to blink back her tears, her cunny tender from the rough treatment with the cane.

'Bring her now!' ordered Desilla, still seething. 'I have several experiments I wish to try on this girl.'

The crowd parted to allow the cart and Babala, who lay helpless upon it, to pass. Desilla led the way, her taut buttocks peeping from beneath the tight black corset and swaying seductively as she walked on the tall heels. The tools that hung like tassels at the lower border of the corset swung rhythmically, tantalisingly, and made Babala quake with trepidation. They looked so fearsome, carefully crafted from polished metal and leather.

'You will probably enjoy Desilla's little games,' whispered Rata, trying to comfort Babala as she fearfully watched Desilla's proud strut down the long passage.

'No,' she said sadly, 'I don't think I will. Desilla does not like me. Indeed, she hates me.'

'It's not that she hates you,' assured Rata. 'She is a little afraid of you, that's all.'

'Afraid of me?' she said incredulously. 'What is it that can possibly make her afraid of me? I am just a weak girl, a slave who must do everything she commands.'

Desilla whipped her head round, her face thunderous, her thighs apart and her hands placed on her hips. 'Oh, yes,' she spat from pursed lips, 'you are pliant enough it is true, but there is a hint of rebelliousness about you that must be driven out before you can be a true slave.'

Pale of face, Babala looked up at Desilla, and her mind ran riot as she tried to imagine what the woman was thinking.

She was soon to find out.

'In my whip case,' said Desilla, 'I have a very pretty collection of playthings,' and trembling, Babala watched as the woman stroked lengths of leather of different thicknesses. 'Your flesh just begs to be caressed by my toys,' she continued. 'It is so smooth and silky...' The woman's dark eyes became positively sultry as she eyed Babala's restrained body, and it was as if she had already forgotten whipping her in the kitchen.

'But before I caress you with my little whips...' Desilla bent from the waist, her eyes narrowed and questioning. 'I shall take you to my bath chamber and have you scrubbed. I know this lowly fellow had you,' she threw a withering glance up at Rata, who looked shamefaced, 'and goodness knows who else before you came here.'

Face aflame, Babala swallowed guiltily. The Slavemaster! Did she know about the Slavemaster - her husband? She surely couldn't. Who could have told her?

'Come along,' ordered Desilla. 'Enough of this idle chatting; I want her in my bath chamber - *now*.' She turned on her spiked heels and strutted swiftly along the passage, and Babala watched that haughty bottom swaying from side to side beneath the leather corset.

Her own buttocks made tender by the rough cart and her limbs aching through the long incarceration in the restraints, Babala sighed. 'Is it much further?' she whispered to Rata, turning her sweet face upwards to look into his eyes.

'No, we are almost there,' he told her, and bent to stroke a wisp of golden hair from her pale cheek before pushing the heavy cart around the corner. The castle was huge, thought

Babala. It was almost as big as the Prince's palace and certainly as luxurious; the Slavemaster must be a very wealthy individual.

'Here we are.' Rata stopped in front of a pair of large oak doors, one of which was ajar.

'Bring her in.' Desilla sounded impatient and imperious. 'And then I want you to go,' she said to Rata. 'Goodness knows what you'd get up to with my girls if I allowed you to stay.'

Light chatter and giggling reached Babala's ears as the cart was pushed into the first chamber of Desilla's quarters. The room was large and clad in polished marble. Girls, dressed as scantily as Babala, watched as Rata pushed the cart into the centre of the floor. The girls, all pretty with a variety of hair and skin colouring, giggled at the sight of the captive.

'Is she very naughty, mistress?' asked one with vibrant red hair.

'Is that why she is chained so tightly?' asked another.

A blonde stroked Rata, tracing the bulge of his biceps and allowed her hands to stray over his hips to the very hem of his tunic. Her dainty fingers were about to dip beneath it to touch his balls and cock, which was beginning to strain upwards.

'Stop that!' snapped Desilla, and the blonde was thrown across the marble floor by a vicious slap. 'And didn't I tell you to get back to the kitchens?' she said, prodding Rata's chest with stiffened fingers. 'Now go - you're a bad influence on my girls.'

As he left the bath chamber Desilla stood over Babala, and beckoned some of the girls closer. 'I want her placed on the examining table,' she said.

'But we might hurt her,' protested the redhead. 'Her restraints are so hard and unyielding and she is already in discomfort.'

'Do as I say,' said Desilla.

The girls were gentle, but the blonde who was slapped could not resist a spiteful pinch of Babala's bottom as she helped to lift her onto the marble table.

'Do you wish us to unfasten her chains now, mistress?' asked the redhead.

'No, not yet,' Desilla said, shaking her head as she eyed her lovely prize. 'Why are you so concerned about her?'

'Because you used me in much the same way when I first arrived here,' the redhead responded, her chin held high.

'And will do so again if I have any more of your cheek,' said Desilla, turning to search a shelf. 'Where is my strainer cup?' she asked, picking up first one implement and then another. 'Have one of you used it?'

'No, mistress,' chorused all the girls.

'We would not presume to take something of yours,' added a girl with hair as black as night. 'And what use would we have for your strainer cup when we rarely see a man?'

'Less of your cheek,' Desilla snapped, before continuing with her search.

'Ah, here it is,' she eventually said, picking up a tube as thick as a large cock. It was made of a hard but clear substance that shone in the candlelight.

The marble was cold and hard beneath Babala's bottom and it struck a chill into her flesh. The manacles rubbed the tender skin at her wrists and ankles and the spacer-rod made her thighs ache.

'Lift her buttocks with this,' Desilla ordered, and the redhead was handed a wooden device, carved to take the fullness of bottom cheeks. The mistress stood, thighs gracefully apart, holding the strainer cup.

'I'll try to be gentle,' whispered the redhead, pushing the wooden pillow beneath Babala's buttocks, and although she was as good as her word, Babala could not help but give a mew of discomfort as the shaped wooden block was pushed beneath her. It was not that the pillow caused her pain; it was the strain it put on the rod and chains that held her captive.

'This will not hurt,' promised Desilla, and the strainer cup, which was not a cup at all but a syringe, was placed at Babala's opening. Desilla pushed forward with the implement and

Babala felt her flesh pouch being pressed open. She parted her lips and gasped.

'Oh, come now,' chivvied the woman. 'You've welcomed many cocks bigger than this, I'm sure. It cannot be hurting for you are slippery as can be; juices seeping very nicely to lubricate your passage.'

'It is hard and cold, mistress,' whispered Babala. 'And it opens me shamefully wide.' She looked up shyly at the girls who watched her humiliation with such interest. 'And they are all staring at my cunny.'

'Stop making a fuss, girl,' sneered Desilla. The strainer cup was fully inserted and Babala felt a sucking sensation that made her draw in her breath. The sucking seemed to go on and on, but at last the strainer cup was withdrawn and Desilla held it to the light of a candle.

'It is full,' Desilla's voice was no more than a whisper. 'And I sucked a great deal from you.' She gave Babala a sideways glance, her eyes narrowed slits of suspicious. 'Rata gave you all this seed?'

Babala said nothing, but wished the floor would swallow her up. Could the syringe be full not only of Rata's issue but Maxim's as well? Was there any way Desilla could know?

'Who else has fucked you?' asked the woman. 'Tell me, who?'

The other girls were silent, huddling together, their soft breasts pressed close and their hands clutched together as if their closeness would give them comfort.

'Well, you little strumpet,' Desilla persisted, 'what have you to say for yourself? Did Rata receive money from a courtier or two for your services as he brought you here? Is that it?' She stroked the iron restraints at Babala's ankles, and then her fingers thrust into the girl's exposed sex. 'They took advantage of your helplessness, I suppose.'

'No, mistress,' murmured Babala, her voice trembling with dread that Desilla might discover the truth; that Maxim had fucked her in the carriage on the way to the castle. She wished she dared wriggle away from the thrusting fingers, but to do so was to invite punishment, she knew.

Desilla sighed and let her fingers slide from Babala's wetness. 'Oh, very well then,' she said, her tone one of irritation. 'But if I ever find out you've put your cunt where you should not...' She drew her forefinger in a cutting movement across her own throat and smiled evilly as she watched Babala shiver.

'Take those restraints from her,' she ordered. 'I have the key.' The redhead reached out to take it, but the dark girl was quicker, and bent down next to Babala.

'It was the master, wasn't it?' she whispered.

Babala darted frightened eyes in Desilla's direction, but the woman was busy at the bench setting out the toys that she unclipped from the lower margin of her corset.

'He does that with all the girl slaves if he gets the chance.' The dark girl kept a wary eye on Desilla as she released the wrist restraints from Babala. 'And madam always suspects, but rarely proves anything.'

'Leave the leg chains in place,' Desilla said suddenly, and the dark girl looked wary, clearly fearing she'd been overheard. 'Lift her into the tub and make sure she is properly scrubbed.'

The girls hurried to do madam's bidding and Babala felt some relief as she was lowered into the warm and perfumed water. Aching and tired from her long restraint in the manacles, she closed her eyes and let her hair float in a golden fan on the milky surface. The girls used perfumed soap and soft cloths to scrub under and over Babala's breasts, paying special attention to the sensitive nipples that sprang up like little pegs.

It was the dark girl who attended to Babala's cunny, made available by the rod that still spread her thighs. 'You have lovely fleshy lips,' she whispered as she dipped into the warm swirling water and soaped Babala's golden curls. Babala said nothing, but the gentle massage was making frissons of pleasure spark within her lower belly, making her feel relaxed, and could not help but moan as her outer lips were peeled open and the dark girl's knowing fingers teased her sensitive nubbin.

'I know what you're up to,' Desilla said, interrupting the moment, and the dark girl yelped and cowered as a whip licked around her slender and bare shoulders. 'I do the pleasuring, not you girls. You have been my body slaves long enough to know that.'

'I am sorry, mistress,' said the girl, 'but her cunny pouts so invitingly.'

'It does, doesn't it?' Desilla purred. 'Take her out. I want her now.'

Babala moved awkwardly in the leg irons, but the girls managed to help her out of the tub and dry her with many soft cloths, and then at last the restraints were unfastened and her legs were free.

'You girls may leave us now,' said Desilla, her predatory eyes fixed on Babala. 'I want her alone. There is much I need to know about this one.' There was a look in her eyes that unnerved Babala. 'Oh, there's no need to look like that,' the woman mused, toying with her prey. 'I have a treat in store before I send you back to the kitchen...'

The girls had gone and the bath chamber echoed with Desilla's next ominous words. 'According to my husband you have been well used before, so what I have planned for you should not be a trial at all.' She strutted towards a door. 'Follow me,' she ordered.

On shaking legs and her mind troubled by the woman's words Babala did as she was told. The room into which she was taken was gloomy and shadowy. It was sparsely furnished with only one narrow table in its centre. Babala looked at Desilla curiously.

'Up on there,' said the woman, 'and spread your arms above your head and part your legs. This is one of my little toys for girls who are disobedient. I punish them.'

'But, mistress, I do everything you say,' Babala protested. 'I try to be good and to please you.'

Desilla's eyes narrowed. 'Hm, when I can see you, but what about when you are out of my sight? What do you get up to then, eh?'

She was talking about her husband, Babala was sure. The cruel woman suspected and this was why she was being punished.

'Up on the table,' Desilla repeated, and gave her a slap on the bottom that made the pert mounds quiver. The sound was like the crack of a whip and hurt almost as much, and Babala stifled a sob of woe. With tears in her eyes she climbed onto the narrow table, opened her legs wide and spread her arms.

'It's quite obvious that you make a habit of making yourself available to all and sundry,' said Desilla, her lips thin and curved in a cruel smile.

'But only because I am made to do so, mistress,' Babala countered bravely, as her wrists were strapped hard to the upper corners of the furniture.

'Don't be impertinent, you little strumpet.'

Babala sighed and wondered exactly what the woman had in store for her - how exactly she was to be tormented.

'This is an interesting device, my sweet.' Desilla stood at her head, looking down at her and fingering a large wheel. 'Since you enjoy to be open and pliant this will make you more so.' She gave a wicked chuckle. 'Very much more so, and will please the gentlemen who are waiting to get their hands on you.'

A click echoed through the bare-walled chamber and Babala felt a tension in her limbs as they were spread wider.

'How does that feel?' asked Desilla.

Babala's breasts felt taut and her nipples stiffened. Her cunny felt extremely exposed, and her sex lips were parted, her clitoris flushed and eager, aching for the touch of a finger or the chafe of a cock. She could sense the drafts in the chamber seeking it out, whispering over the golden curls and meandering like an icy stream over the heated inner flesh. 'It feels very strange, mistress,' she admitted, although privately she thought how deliciously vulnerable she felt.

'Stretched, would you say?' probed Desilla.

'Very much so, mistress,' said Babala. Her sex bud did indeed feel stretched, making the tension in her limbs feel as nothing of any great importance.

'It will feel even more so by the time my gentlemen friends have finished with you,' Desilla threatened. 'And then you will hold no appeal for my straying husband whatsoever.' She smiled maliciously. 'You will not know who they are, of course. No, that wouldn't do at all. They will be masked.' She gave the wheel at Babala's head another turn and the girl felt her belly hollow from the extra tension, felt her breasts become flatter on her ribs and felt her legs become more open. 'Only I will know that.'

Babala moaned, finding it more difficult to breathe as she was stretched, but despite her anxiety she felt her sex sap seep generously, warm and milky, trickling over her folds and soaking through her golden pussy curls. She twisted her head to look at the Slavemaster's wife and cringed from the disturbingly intense expression in the dark eyes.

It was a trick - Babala knew it. Desilla was taunting her. She'd known all the time that Maxim had seduced her in the carriage. The rack and the masked men, they were all a ploy to tease and torture Babala. Not to make her unappealing to the woman's husband in the future, but to punish her for acts already perpetrated. And at the end of it all she would be condemned to a life as a serving wench in the kitchens, or horror of all horrors - thrown from the crag to an awful death.

Desilla's expression changed. She became bright and inviting as she moved away and opened the heavy oak double doors. 'Come in, gentlemen,' she beckoned, smoothing the supple leather of her tight corset over her shapely body. 'The girl is prepared, and I know you will all enjoy her immensely.'

Four men - aristocrats, judging by their expensively heavy cloaks - crowded into the room. Macabre carnival masks hid their faces, turning them into grotesque demons, and behind the masks eyes glinted avariciously. Babala could hear their breathing, harsh and rapid, eager and wanting - and somehow this increased her treacherous yearning. The Taskmaster's training had been extremely thorough; she could feel the greater pulse of her sex bud and its growing heat. Her limbs, stretched and secured as they were, only served to increase her shameful excitement.

'Perhaps you would care to open your codpieces, gentlemen,' Desilla offered. 'I am sure our dear girl would love to see what is in store for her.'

The cloaks were swept aside and codpieces, the padded covers that enhanced the men's groins, were unfastened and erections of varying length and girth sprang forth. They were already proud and turgid, the knobs bared and shiny, slippery with pre-issue. The men remained silent and stood in line, waiting their turn to ravage Babala.

As her sapphire eyes traveled along the display of swollen members she readied herself for the onslaught. A strange pride made her look at each of the men in turn, and watch as they blatantly stroked their rigid stems, glossing their issue over their bulbous helmets.

'You,' Desilla broke the hush that blanketed the ghoulish scene, pushing forward the heavily built man nearest to her. 'Will it be you first? Yes, I think you are a good choice. Take your turn with her. She is well prepared, as you can see. There will be no resistance.'

'She looks too innocent to know how to please a man thoroughly,' grumbled the man, but despite his objection he moved closer to Babala and began to thumb her inflamed clitoris, and she whispered her pleasure and strained to lift her hips to the man's touch.

'Well, believe me,' said Desilla, with a cynical smile, 'she is not, as you can see by her wanton reaction.'

Without any more hesitation the man climbed onto the table, and Babala could hear him grunting with anticipated pleasure, and hear him panting with effort as he settled between her thighs.

'You are right, madam,' he enthused. 'She could not remain innocent with such an appealing cunt.'

Babala felt tears fill her eyes at this humiliating statement. She felt her cheeks flame, but still her sex felt proud and ready.

'She says she was trained,' Desilla sneered scathingly. 'By someone called the Taskmaster, in Ellipsis. But my dear husband acquired her more cheaply than he could a whore.' She stroked her darkly curled mound in a thoughtful manner. 'A whore,' she repeated, and hissed the word as she looked at Babala's spread thighs and the man who had settled between them.

Babala, held fast by the manacles at the head and foot of the table, her mound thrust up by the tautness of the restraints, looked stoically through her tears into the eyes behind the fearsome mask, trying to give no hint of pain or dread.

To the man she was a gloriously inviting and passive beauty. 'Now, my sweet,' he grunted from behind the mask, 'you will enjoy my pleasuring.'

'Where are your manners, girl?' snapped Desilla. 'Answer the gentleman.' She turned the wheel at Babala's head another notch, but she made no murmur of complaint.

Babala felt the smooth thickness of a cock at her entrance, felt the push as he spread her. The force of his cock pulled upon her clitty hood, baring it and making it available to be chafed by the in and out thrust of his thickness. She could not help but mew with pleasure as thrills circled around her lower belly like a whirlpool within her body. The increased stretching she felt at her arms and legs were as nothing as her cunny was opened to the full.

The other men murmured appreciatively at her sounds of pleasure and pressed forward to watch the spectacle of her fucking more closely.

'You see how she glories in her helplessness,' hissed Desilla. 'There is no hint of panic as there would be in a normal girl.

There is only pride in her openness and vulnerability, and see how she parts her moist lips in invitation.' She fingered her breasts where they spilled from the upper margins of the waist-whittling corset.

Babala clutched the big man's cock with her soft cunny walls as her ecstasy mounted and he grunted more loudly. 'Tell me what you want me to do,' he rasped. 'Tell me crudely!'

'I - I want you to fuck me,' said Babala, in a soft and inviting voice. 'I want to feel your cockstem pulsing within me and I want to feel your seed, hot and creamy, washing the walls of my sex.'

'Oh, too much! She speaks the crude words so sexily. I cannot hold back, Desilla.'

'Then let it go,' the woman urged. 'Let your come flood her. Don't hold back.'

A passion gripped Babala as the smooth heat of his cockstem nestled within her clutching folds, and her fluids soaked the invading shaft and she felt the first burst of his seed. The several fountains were copious and hot. Babala's own orgasm flowed through her like a spiral that lifted her up and she squeezed the cock until the last drop was milked from him.

'Oh, excellent!' crowed Desilla, watching the man's heavy body slumped upon Babala's shapely form. 'Now get off her.'

With some difficulty the man clambered from Babala's body, his mask a little awry upon his sweating face. 'The girl is a witch, Desilla,' he said in no more than a breathless whisper. 'She drains a man's strength.'

'Oh, what nonsense,' Desilla scoffed. 'She merely drained your seed, and you will remain grateful to me for allowing it.' She pushed the man away from the table upon which Babala lay so helplessly.

'Let us carry on.' She looked along the line of men, giving their cocks more than cursory glances, and chose the next. Babala surmised by his slender physique that he was young, although his cock was longer and thicker than the previous man's.

'Make this fucking last,' ordered Desilla, giving the first man a withering glance. 'She got away too easily with the first one.'

Needful, thought Babala; her flesh was needful. It was as the Taskmaster told her it would be. She would be able to take one man and then more men and enjoy them all. She wanted the young man's cock to slide into the silky depths of her vagina; although her body was chained and helpless, her vagina was free and willing.

The young man smoothed his fingers up and down her parted thighs with a touch that made her flesh tremble with delight. He caressed her belly and stroked the puff of golden curls on her mound, and thumbed the full pad of flesh at the very apex of her cunny.

'Oh, get on with it,' Desilla intervened impatiently, so the young man hastily lowered between Babala's thighs and stroked the length of his cock up and down her slit, coating himself with her juices. It nudged the tip of her nubbin, and he groaned and fumbled his cock into her opening. Such was his length and the slowness of his entry that Babala thought she would faint away with the pleasure it gave her.

'Get on with it!' the Slavemaster's wife repeated angrily. 'You know what I want to see; I want to see something which thrills me in my whoring chamber and so far you have done nothing but bore me. I want to be stimulated by what you do to the girl! Understand?'

The bizarre group grunted behind their masks and the young man immediately drove his cock deep inside Babala. His strokes were slow and rhythmic, and his rigid length had a throbbing power that made the trussed girl swoon.

'Let me feel her,' Desilla ordered, and Babala felt the Slavemaster's wife sit upon the edge of the table, could feel her bare buttocks against her own straining thigh.

The young man plunged into her and his balls slapped against her buttocks.

'Good...' murmured Desilla, and her ringed fingers slid between the couple to finger the root of the pistoning cock and feel the spread flesh leaves of Babala's cunny. It was both humiliating and exciting to Babala. She felt the woman's fingers squeezing her open yet further to feel the man's cock deep within her. 'More,' ordered the Slavemaster's wife. 'I want to feel the movement of your cock within the little strumpet.' Although she'd demanded a longer coupling this time, her caressing of the man's cock was too much for him to bear, and with one final grunt he came and flooded not only Babala's cunny, but also coated Desilla's probing fingers.

'Oh, *really*,' Desilla frowned as she pulled them from Babala's cunny. 'I told you to pace yourself!'

'It was your fingers, mistress,' the young man protested, defending his lack of staying prowess. 'It was too much stimulation for any man to bear.'

Wiping her hands upon a strip of silk, Desilla waved a dismissive hand. Then her eyes narrowed as she looked at the last two waiting men. 'You,' she said, deciding upon one of them. 'Come here.'

The man confidently flung off the robe he wore, and she gasped to see that his wonderfully toned body was oiled to show the sculptured contours of honed muscle. He had a slim waist although he was mature, much like the Taskmaster. His cock stood from his body like the spear that it was. The balls were trimmed of hair so that they were smooth to the touch. These and his cock were oiled too, and he allowed his fist to slide up and down the spear of flesh and cup his balls.

But there was something about this man that was not only familiar but also intensely unsettling, and had Babala been able she would have fled the room. Her eyes flitted anxiously to Desilla.

'Well, fine sir,' the woman said huskily. 'You have spent a great deal of time preparing your body, and in particular, your penis. Do you not wish to insert it into our young *slave* here?'

It seemed to Babala that Desilla put great emphasis on the word slave, but despite her trepidation it somehow caused her an extra thrill.

The smooth and oiled body lay upon the trembling girl. The slippery globe was positioned without any fumbling at her entrance, but even though well lubricated it was necessary for the mysterious owner to grind his hips energetically to obtain entry because of the dimensions of the organ. Babala gasped as she was opened, and the man's hands grasped her shoulders to gain purchase and to lever her helpless body as he pushed ever inwards. Her sex was fully opened, and her bud was exposed to the rubbing of his immense cock.

Then he drew back and sat on his heels, his cock standing upright from his groin and gleaming with the rich essence of Babala's pearly dew. Tenderly, he pressed open her love lips, exposing her slippery inner leaves.

'What are you doing?' Desilla demanded impatiently. 'She is a mere slave; why are you so intent on giving her pleasure?'

The mask turned upon Desilla, but he said nothing; he was more absorbed in driving two thick fingers into Babala's smooth opening while his thumbs slithered over the tip of her throbbing clitoris.

'Didn't you hear me?' Desilla persisted, her anger intensifying while Babala moaned as his attentions sent her in a spiral of ecstasy. As she came she heard the man groan his own pleasure and saw his spume erupt from his throbbing penis to splash on her shuddering breasts and belly.

'No!' screamed Desilla, her venomous mood becoming dangerously intense. 'You knew I wanted her fucked beyond endurance by each of you. You *knew!*'

But the man threw back his head, his dark hair glossed with sweat, and laughed uproariously.

Chapter 8

Babala was dragged by her hair to the kitchen, along the dark narrow stone passages. Her body ached from the rough usage it had received for so many hours.

'You will work in the kitchens for the rest of your days,' hissed the servant in whose charge she now was. 'That is what my mistress said and we, the cooks and the scullery men, may use you as the mood takes us.'

Babala lifted her hands to the roots of her golden hair to try and ease the excruciating tension. The man who took such delight in teasing both her and Desilla was Maxim, the Slavemaster, of that Babala was convinced. How he had the gall to do such a thing right in front of his awesome wife she knew not. And how Desilla had not recognised him at least until it was too late poor bewildered Babala also couldn't understand. But it was him, she was sure. The cock was so long and thick, deliciously smooth, the globe large. She shuddered at the thought of it opening her sex to push into her tightness.

'You were a fool to displease the mistress,' said the servant, resting for a moment in the chilly stone passageway. He stroked the pouting cushions of her bottom, making her kneel on all fours on the flagstone floor so he could examine them more fully in the flickering light of a sconce. 'Such a tight rear cleft,' he murmured, using both hands to ease her buttocks apart. 'And such a darling rear pit...'

Babala felt the servant's finger press open the tiny pleats and could not help the shiver of longing which rippled through her weary body. Those brutish guards had first breached that opening, and she could not help remembering not only the discomfort but also the soaring bliss.

'It is moist,' remarked the servant.

'The dew is from my cunny, sir,' Babala said honestly. 'It trickled down the cleft.'

'Perhaps we should add a little more,' suggested the servant, and she felt his fingers probe into the soft depths of her sex, seeking the slippery dew. She bore back upon the intrusion, instinctively helping him, and felt additional sap seep from her folds. 'Good,' grunted the servant. 'You are going to be very popular in the kitchen.'

The fingers slithered back between her buttocks and massaged the creamy juices into her rear bud. Babala felt it give under the pressure, and the servant lifted his brief tunic to show his cockstem. She knew it was a compliment to her that it was fully bloated, with the veins bulging in a tight trail along its length. The end globe was shiny and slick with seed, and the servant was looking at her hungrily, fingering her rear bud with one hand and stroking his turgid length with the other.

'You will allow me to enter your fine bottom,' he croaked, his tongue lolling around his wet slack lips.

Babala sighed. 'I can do no other, sir,' she said, 'for I am a slave to the whole castle.'

'But you enjoy it.' The servant sunk the tip of his forefinger into her rear opening and she could not help but bear up to his touch. It was true - she did enjoy it. The Taskmaster had taught her well: to be submissive and pliant to everyone and anyone who sought her services. The finger drove into her tight darkness to the hilt, and the pressure of its entry caused her nubbin to pulse excitedly in response. She could not help but writhe sensuously on her hands and knees, seeking relief from the shameful desire that flooded her.

'Oh, yes,' said the servant, plunging the finger back and forth. 'You enjoy it. Would you enjoy my cock flushing that tightness now?'

'If... if it would please you, sir.'

The servant fell upon her and she felt his slippery bulb trying to gain entry into her tight rear. He slid a hand round to cup the fullness of her sex and open her lips so that his fingers could stroke her yearning sex bud, and as he pleasured the throbbing little morsel of flesh he was able to ease into her rear opening. Babala felt the pressure, felt the slide as her own sap greased his thickness, and sighed a little moan of pleasure as his entry became deeper and her ecstasy grew in intensity... but then she froze as they were interrupted by Maxim's resonant tones.

The frantic servant pulled out and drew back, muttering incoherent apologies to his master as his seed spilling in involuntary spurts while he struggled to his feet. Babala looked up from beneath her golden fringe, wondering if she was to be punished yet again, but too weary to care.

Maxim towered above them. His silken robe was open, and Babala's eyes were drawn up the honed strength of his legs to the smoothness of his balls and the upright stance of his turgid cock.

'Did you hear me?' he repeated, making no effort to hide his manhood. 'What is going on here? This girl may be a slave to be used by the kitchen staff, but not in a public place.' His face was suffused with anger and his cock seemed to rear up as if to echo that anger.

'Beg pardon, s-sir,' grovelled the servant, bowing and scraping. 'I-I misunderstood.'

Maxim bent to pull Babala to her feet, and she hung her head until he lifted her dainty chin with a forefinger. 'I want to fuck you again,' he said quietly. 'But you must be cleansed before I will put my cock where this fellow has been.'

'In the mistress's bath house?' Babala asked humbly.

'No,' he decided. 'I shall take you to my own bath chamber. My feelings for Desilla and her cruelty grow less as the hours pass, whereas for you my feelings grow.'

The servant had gone, slinking away into the shadows, and Maxim led her to his own quarters.

A heavy perfume hung in the air, making her feel dreamy and heavy-limbed. Channels carved into the stone walls carried the aroma and wisps of it caressed Babala's naked body like insubstantial fingers, pampering her until she thought she would swoon with delight in Maxim's arms.

He handed her over to a small and dowdy woman. 'Be gentle with her,' he instructed, but make sure she is thoroughly cleansed.'

Babala felt afraid when Maxim left, for there was something about the small woman that unsettled her.

'On the bench,' said the woman, and once again Babala was made to climb upon a table. The woman was rough as she stretched Babala's arms above her head and she felt the cold hardness of iron manacles clipped about her wrists. She was face down and her legs were spread to the full. Maxim had seemed so caring, and yet he had left her in the hands of a woman who seemed to like nothing better than to be cruel.

'Why?' murmured Babala. 'Why are you doing this? I have done nothing to you.'

'Maxim's orders,' came the clipped reply, and any further response from the girl was drenched by a deluge of icy-cold water that made her gasp and caught her words in her throat. Another and another followed until she could scarcely breathe and shivered miserably.

'You girls have it too easy,' said the spiteful servant, putting the third empty bucket on the wet floor as Babala thought how unfair her words were; she would hardly call what she had suffered at Desilla's hands easy.

'Why are you being so harsh with me?' she asked again, her voice quiet and pitiful.

The woman sniffed and went about her tasks. 'Orders,' she said sharply. 'That's all. I have nothing against you personally.' She stroked the fullness of Babala's buttocks and her touch had a strange wistfulness about it. The cold made Babala feel stiff, and when she tried to lift her head to look at the woman she could not. The fetters held her still on the narrow bench, and she could do nothing but listen as the woman moved about the room collecting items, which she laid by her captive's shivering thighs.

Fingers prised open Babala's rear opening and she felt oil being dripped around the tightness. The oil was warm and the feeling was almost unbearably sensual, especially when the woman massaged her sex with the slick ointment.

Then, not unexpectedly, Babala felt a pressure against her rear and something firm sank deep into the dark passage. She shivered in anticipation of more pleasurable sensations, clutching the invasive item with her rectum. The same was done to her vagina and she could not help but bear down to increase the wanton feeling the phallic pressure gave her. She tried to writhe instinctively and heard the woman cackle with evil laughter at her attempted movement.

'The tubes are for the purpose of flushing you out,' said the woman, and cackled again as though she had said something hilariously funny. 'And from what I hear that is something you require badly.' The snigger died and the woman's tone became spiteful once more. 'Once I have poured the cleansing fluid into you the tubes will be removed and you must retain it until I give you permission to release it.'

A flood of warmth entered Babala's body, and she couldn't suppress a pleasurable sigh. Then the tubes were withdrawn and she contracted her muscles to keep the perfumed soapy fluid within her. Never had she been so glad of the Taskmaster's strict training, for she knew that had she not been taught the fluids would have quickly seeped from her to spill on the bench. She shuddered as she imagined what punishments would be rained down upon her had she released the liquids.

'Hold...' hissed the woman, cupping Babala's sex in her hand, and to the girl's shame she felt her nubbin swelling as the fluids swirled within her, bringing pressure to bear and making it difficult to concentrate.

'This is good, my dear,' said the woman, and her finger tickled the tip of Babala's nubbin. 'Now you can let your pleasure flow and let me feel your sex bud jerk upon my finger.' The harshness of only moments before was replaced by tender urging, and Babala could not help but welcome her orgasm, her brow furrowed as she strove to hold onto the soothing liquids while she savoured her blissful release.

'Now,' whispered the woman, bending to stroke Babala's wet hair from her ear, 'now you can let the fluids go, let them pulse out in the rhythm of your come,' and with a shudder of relief Babala relaxed and felt the fluids wash from her vagina and from her bowel, onto the table, from where they cascaded to the floor.

The fetters were released from her ankles and wrists and Babala was turned over. The woman's fingers petted her taut chilled breasts and Babala winced as her nipples were coaxed to erection. Her full sex lips were parted and caressed, and then with harsh lips her clitoris was kissed and sucked.

'You lucky girl,' the woman rasped. 'You don't know how lucky you are.'

'W-why?' Babala whispered, hating but loving the woman's cold touch. 'Why do you say that?'

'Once I was a beauty,' said the woman, 'sought after by Maxim and his courtiers.'

'And... and what happened?' Babala asked, her eyes closed against the ongoing torment, fearing the answer. Warm oil was dribbled over her tummy and breasts as the woman began to massage her flesh in soothing circles. Her breasts received lingering attention, and then the golden fleece on her sex mound was gently preened until she thought she would faint with pleasure. 'What happened?' she asked again, dreamily as her belly was massaged in slow circles.

'I was a virgin when I was brought here,' said the woman, 'and Maxim was having one of his lavish parties. The guests were very drunk and I was given to a man who was almost insensible with alcohol.'

The luxurious oil with which Babala was massaged was richly perfumed and made her sex folds especially sensitive. It was heady and she could scarcely concentrate on what the woman was saying.

'He became angry when his cock would not rise to his command,' the woman continued. 'In the end he brought many of Maxim's guests to service me so that he could watch. They came upon me time after time until I thought I would die.'

The massage continued and Babala almost drifted into sleep, but as the tale reached its conclusion she opened her eyes. 'How terrible,' she sympathised, remembering how beautiful the taking of her own virginity was at the hands of the Taskmaster. 'What did you do?'

'I ran away.'

'Down the crag?'

'There was a gatekeeper. He helped me, but I was so weak after my ordeal I had not the strength to carry on.'

'So you were brought back and punished?'

The woman's voice, despite her awful tale, was soothing, as were her hands. They strayed to the proud plumpness of Babala's mound, petting it and stroking the golden curls now gleaming with oil. The touch was firm, but so sensual that Babala could not help but bear up to receive more stimulation. Seeing what was needed her sex lips were spread and a thumb balled the aching tip of her sex bud. Babala gasped as, once more, hot breath washed over her revealed sex and a moist tongue lapped eagerly at her clitoris.

But Babala was not prepared for what came next. 'My punishment was a final humiliation.' The woman's voice was soft and muffled as she spoke against Babala's sex flesh.

'What did they do?' She knew Desilla was over fond of the whip and eager to use it on naked and vulnerable flesh whenever an opportunity arose. It seemed to Babala that it pleasured Desilla to hear the crack of it across an upturned bottom or around a slender waist.

'They circumcised me,' the woman said frankly, her teeth nibbling Babala's clitoris and two fingers slipping into the taut passage of her cunny.

'No!' croaked Babala, horrified, but despite her horror her body was gripped by intensely blissful convulsions. Her orgasm was strong and seemed to go on and on as though it would never end.

'W-will they do that to me?' she asked fearfully when she regained her breath and the waves of ecstasy had subsided.

The woman shrugged indifferently. 'Who knows? Maxim seems to have taken a great liking to you, but Desilla... who knows what she might do to you? Some say she is mad - crazy with jealousy when anyone threatens her position here.'

The two females said nothing more as the servant sponged away the oil with sweet smelling soap and patted Babala dry.

Babala's hair was brushed into a shimmering and golden cascade and the bush on her cunny was fluffed into soft curls.

'You know how Maxim likes you to stand?' asked the woman, helping Babala down from the bench, who nodded and bowed her head submissively.

'That's good,' the woman decreed. 'If you make sure you please Maxim you should be safe here, but we must hurry for he will be preparing for the banquet.'

Babala was hurried along the shadowy passages until they came to Maxim's chambers.

'Were you tended and cleansed properly?' he asked, cupping her breasts and stroking the silken skin.

Babala nodded and shuddered as he allowed his hand to drift over the pout of her belly and down to the soft bed of curls between her thighs, and it seemed only natural to shuffle her feet a little further apart to give him easier access to her cunny.

She heard him sigh as his fingers stroked her inner lips and parted them to touch the very tip of her nubbin, and the pleasure this gave her drove the awful thoughts of what could happen to her at the hands of Desilla from her mind. She ground against his hand, rubbing against the palm as his fingers slid in and out of her slippery vagina.

'You wish me to fuck you, my dear,' he stated. 'You wish me to fill you with my seed.'

Babala nodded, for the power of the man reminded her of the Taskmaster, and she could not resist him. Her very helplessness made her a prisoner, no matter what the consequences, but the threat of a jealous and furious Desilla still lurked somewhere in the back of her mind.

Maxim pulled her to a damask couch and sat with his cock rising, huge and magnificently rigid from his groin. 'Straddle me, my dear,' he said huskily, 'and sink your soft and willing flesh around me.'

Even though she trembled uncontrollably she was still drawn to him, and her sex flesh was moist with desire. She sank down slowly, keeping her thighs tense and open, supporting herself upon her bent knees. His globe, thick and smooth, pushed her labia fully open and, as she slid onto him, she felt his fingers glancing over the tip of her clitty. His free hand held her hip, guiding her down upon him. She petted his long length with her sex lips, and heard him groan in ecstasy.

She must escape, she knew, even as her orgasm sent her soaring to a momentary heaven, even as he erupted into her depths. Somehow she must escape, from the castle, and from the threat of Desilla.

When their coupling was over he kissed her fondly, stroked her cheek with the tip of his thumb and looked into her eyes with an expression that was both sad and tender. 'I must return you to the kitchen,' he said, and she could feel his breath on her cheek as he spoke. 'The banquet is due to start soon and I need you to entertain my guests.'

Babala lowered her eyes modestly. 'Entertain, sir?'

'Hm, that beautiful cunt of yours will make many of my guests, both men and women, very happy.'

'Whatever pleases you, sir,' she said obediently, but her heart was heavy. Once more she was to be used as a plaything and then looked down upon as a whore.

Maxim clapped his hands, and from the shadows emerged a very large, fearfully ugly man. 'Take her to the kitchens and Rata will give her my orders,' the Slavemaster ordered him. 'And no one is to touch her again before tonight's gathering. Do you understand me? No one. I want her fully responsive and attentive where my guests are concerned...' and with that Babala was dismissed.

The servant gripped her upper arm and led her from the room, and she dared not struggle for the hold upon her was like a vice and he was formidably strong.

'The master used you well,' the big man said gruffly as they traipsed along the winding passageways towards the kitchens, and Babala felt her cheeks tinge pink with shame at the truth of what he said.

'I cannot have a woman,' he added morosely, a few minutes later.

'Why not?' she asked.

'Because...' the poor man looked so sad, '...because I am so ugly. Ever since I was a child many, many years ago, people told me no female would ever be interested in me - would never want to bed me. And so it has proved...'

'Come now,' Babala said sweetly, trying to lighten his mood, not liking to see one so obviously lonely, 'I'm sure that's not true.'

The big man shook his head gloomily. 'Oh, but it is. I've never felt the joys of a woman's touch. Never felt sweet lips around my cock. Never penetrated a woman's sex...'

'Well, that may be so, but - '

'Would you be nice to me then?' he suddenly pressed, stopping and turning to look earnestly into her eyes.

The abruptness of the question caught Babala off guard, and she searched for the right words to say without hurting him further. She'd been through enough and had a daunting evening ahead, so she had few emotions to spare for the poor man.

'No, of course you wouldn't,' he concluded, shaking his head and turning to lead her on.

Long minutes passed and they walked in silence. His shoulders were hunched and her pity for the gentle giant increased tenfold.

'Wait,' she said before she could stop herself. 'Come here,' and she gave him a cuddle, her arms barely reaching round to his back. In the dingy passageway they stood quietly together like that for a few minutes, Babala with her cheek pressed against his broad chest, surprised at the intense sympathy and affection she suddenly felt for the man. 'I... I will be nice to you,' she whispered carefully, feeling something trunk-like swelling against her tummy, 'if you really want me to.'

But the man shook his head. 'No, you don't really want to. You're just trying to be nice to a pathetic, ugly wretch.'

'No,' Babala insisted. 'You're not ugly and you're not a wretch. I think you're probably a very kind and very gentle man.' She looked over her shoulder and saw a shadowy alcove behind her. 'Come,' she whispered, pulling his hands. 'Come,' and she guided him back into the shadowy privacy of the tiny recess.

Words were now unnecessary, so she reached for the hem of his tunic and slowly lifted it, and his rising penis sprung free, bobbing against her tummy. The look of sheer disbelief etched on the lonely man's face made her heart weep for him in sympathy.

He breathed heavily, watching spellbound as one delicate hand let go of the tunic and hovered, and then cool fingers curled around his rigid stalk and he gasped hoarsely. 'Oh, little miss...' he sighed.

'Shhh...' whispered Babala, lifting easily up onto tiptoe to place a gentle kiss on his dry lips. 'Don't say another word,' and then she gave him a little smile of encouragement and sank down again, but further, gracefully down to her knees, and despite his size he shuddered like a timid boy, not quite knowing what to expect. His huge chest heaved as his breath faltered in his throat, and his stout arms dangled uselessly by his sides.

'Would you like me to go on?' she whispered sweetly, and he nodded dumbly, looking down with incredulity at her angelic, upturned face.

Her lips parted slightly and hovered as she looked at the spear of flesh pulsing before her face. The cool fingers tightened around him, and then she leaned closer, her lips parted further, and his erection pressed into the warmth of her welcoming mouth. The man groaned and allowed her fist to pull him ever closer, until he nudged the back of her throat and her fingers only had room to wrap around the very root of him.

His hands cupped her head and stroked it with surprising tenderness, and Babala felt him swelling further inside her mouth. She sucked and licked as best she could, desperately wanting to please the gentle giant.

He groaned above her, gazing down at the lustrously golden head held against his groin, moving gently within his grip, the unseen tongue and lips working beautifully to give him pleasures the like of which he'd never dreamed he would or could ever experience. And the sweet suckling sound, rising up to him in unison with the caresses of her mouth, only served to heighten his joy, and before long he knew his orgasm was imminent.

Babala knew it too, and steeled herself for the years of pent-up frustration to deluge her mouth and throat. She swallowed his full length and reached beneath his tunic with both hands to cup his muscular buttocks, and held him close, wanting him to use her mouth as he wanted.

'Ohhh, little miss...' he groaned, and then his erection swelled even further, its girth making her jaw ache and cheeks hollow, and his seed burst forth copiously. Babala swallowed diligently, her nostrils flared and her breasts moulding against his stocky thighs as she breathed deeply, determined to make it an experience the man would never forget, and then his penis spent again, filling her mouth and making her throat work hard to accept his creamy emission.

Gradually his passion ebbed and his flesh began to soften between her lips. Babala let go of his buttocks and eased back onto her heels, his flesh slipping from the haven of her mouth, a little drop of his seed dripping onto her breast, where it shimmered like a pearl in the half-light.

'Oh, little miss,' he sighed again, bending to help her to her feet, 'thank you. I never knew such delights were possible. And even if I did know, I would never have dreamed they would ever pay me a visit. I will never forget what you have given me...'

Feeling a little light-headed, Babala touched a fingertip to the big man's lips. 'Shhh...' she whispered. 'Next time we'll go a little further...' she added, and her eyes sparkled mischievously in the shadows as understanding crept onto his face and made him smile conspiratorially.

'Then I cannot wait for the next time,' he beamed. 'And if I can ever help you, my little angel... if you ever need me, I will do all I can to be there. You have only to call and I will come - wherever you are.'

Babala, her legs a little weak with the excitement of giving the man so much pleasure, and from the memory of the feel of his potent manhood in her mouth, laid her golden head on his immense chest. 'Thank you,' she murmured.

'No, my little angel,' he said softly as he held her tight, 'it is I who should thank you.' He lowered his face and kissed the top of her head as he stroked a fingertip down the perfection of her cheek. 'No one has ever given me anywhere near as much as you have just given me. You didn't have to, you know.'

Babala closed her eyes and relaxed in the security of his powerful embrace. 'I know I didn't,' she said. 'But I wanted to do it for you.'

With the same gentle finger that stroked her cheek the man lifted her chin, looking into her wide blue eyes. 'Is there anything I can do for you, little miss?' he asked. 'You have only to ask.'

Looking up into his kind face, Babala could not help but think of what Maxim and his formidable wife might do if either of them found out about their little indiscretion - particularly after Maxim's warning that she was to remain untouched until the evening festivities - and she couldn't help but worry for him. Despite the warmth of his body a shiver ran down her spine. She rested her cheek back against the comforting strength of his chest. 'What will they do to you if they discover what we have done?' she murmured against his tunic.

'They will not,' he stated determinedly.

'They might,' Babala insisted anxiously. 'And they might punish you severely.' With a trembling hand she reached beneath his tunic and stroked the semi-turgid fullness of his cock. 'Desilla, I am sure, would take great delight in teasing this before taking it from you.'

His complexion paled as the implications of her words sunk in. 'Then, what do you suggest, little miss? You are as unsafe as I am.'

Babala shivered again and allowed his cock to fall gently back between his strong thighs, her mind made up. 'I think we should both flee this awful place before they find out what we have done.' She glanced up and down the dingy passageway, her own paranoia suddenly making her very frightened. 'If they haven't already...'

'But we are slaves,' he countered. 'Maxim and Desilla own us.'

'What could they do to us for trying to escape that could be any worse than what they might do if they discover what we've done together? What could they do that would be any worse than our lives now?'

He nodded, absorbing the truth of her words. 'But there will be many dangers as we make our way down the crag. Many dangers.' He shook his head and his face was creased with worry. 'And that's if we even get out of the castle.'

'What is your name?' Babala asked.

'Huru,' he said simply.

'Then we shall have to face any dangers together, Huru,' she told him defiantly.

Chapter 9

Desilla, dressed in a gown made of the finest black leather, strode about the kitchen, flailing her whip at any poor unfortunate within range. Her breasts were bare and pert, probing their fullness through carefully cut circles. Silver rings pierced her taut nipples and caught the dim light thrown out from the huge range and the candles set into niches cut into the stone walls.

The gown was slit from the flowing hem to Desilla's crotch. As she strode about the busy room the lush curls of her pussy bush could clearly be seen, but none of the kitchen staff made a comment nor turned their eyes in that direction.

'Where is that girl?' she demanded, of no one in particular. 'She is the entertainment for the banquet.' Her face distorted with anger and she lashed out viciously with the whip, catching Rata around his shoulders, but he managed to remain upright, showing little of the acute pain he felt. Desilla, her anger quelled for the moment, picked up a root vegetable, scrubbed and peeled. 'My guests would delight to see the little strumpet plunge this and other fruits of the earth into her cunny.' She stroked the tip of the vegetable across her parted lips, caressing it with her tongue. 'Come here, Rata,' she ordered slyly.

Understanding her spiteful intent he did not cower, for he knew that was what Desilla delighted in. So he moved, his back straight and head held high, towards his cruel mistress.

Maxim met his wife at the door of the great dining hall. 'You have been a long time, my dear,' he said, and despite the endearment she could tell he was angry.

'You sent me to look for the girl,' she reminded him, 'and I am afraid, dear husband, that she is nowhere to be seen.'

The revellers were all seated at the long tables. They were already noisy with wine, but their chatter stopped as their host and hostess entered the hall.

'I am greatly sorry to disappoint you ladies and gentlemen,' Maxim announced, 'but our entertainment for the evening, the beauty called Babala, seems to have disappeared.' The assembled guests muttered with disappointment and mugs of swilling ale were banged on the table, but Maxim merely smiled and held up his hands for silence. 'However, we have a gracious volunteer to take her place,' he added.

Desilla felt his hand grip hers in an iron hold. 'Did you enjoy yourself with our servants, my dear?' he hissed in her ear. 'Degrading the family name and belittling our station in the kitchens?'

'H-how do you - ?'

'How do I know?' Maxim cut in. He grabbed a kitchen maid who had been trembling behind him, her eyes wide with fear, and Desilla felt her own complexion drain.

Maxim's lips curled into a sneering smile. 'I see your memory serves you well, my dear.' He threw the girl from him and she cried out as her bottom caught the edge of a table and she was swamped by three of the guests, who began to slobber and maul her.

Head held high, Desilla turned on her heels and began to make for the door, but she took only two strides before the crack of a whip echoed around the great hall and she howled with pain, shock and indignation.

'Come back here,' Maxim growled, his voice more fierce than she had ever heard it. 'Since I presume you have much to do with my beautiful Babala's disappearance,' he accused, gripping her upper arm and wrenching her back against his chest, 'you must take her place.' He laughed, and the laughter made Desilla's heart sink.

'T-take her place?' She could feel every contour of his body, could feel his cock rigid against his stomach, and knew he was greatly excited at the prospect of her degradation before the assembled guests.

'Yes, my darling wife,' he sneered, already unfastening the buttons down the front of her gown until it slipped apart and slid from her pale shoulders, leaving her naked apart from her high-heeled ankle boots.

Chapter 10

Babala shivered in the chill of the night air and her new friend and ally clutched her to him as they walked, a sturdy arm squeezing her shoulders reassuringly.

'Where are you going with that girl?' demanded a guard, who stood on the drawbridge of the castle.

Even in the moonlit gloom Babala saw him stare hungrily at her body, and was so grateful for the presence of Huru.

'I have orders to throw her over the crag,' he said.

'What a waste,' grumbled the guard, licking his fat lips. 'Who would know if I took my pleasure before you do it, Huru?' He cast his large colleague a fleeting questioning glance, but his piggy eyes quickly returned to crawl all over the lovely girl.

'I would,' said Huru, holding Babala closer, 'but - '

'What harm would it do?' the guard cut in, his tunic now fully lifted and his cock rigid and throbbing in his hands. 'Just give me a few minutes with her... come on, my friend.'

Babala snuggled closer into Huru's trunk-like arms, but still felt anxious.

'If she's going over the crag anyway,' the guard persisted, 'it won't matter what we do to her. You and I could have our fill of her and no one would ever know any different.'

'I would know,' said Huru. 'Now leave us be.'

But not to be put off such a rare and tasty treat so easily, the guard raised his pike threateningly and aimed it at Huru's face. 'You're planning on having the whore for yourself,' he accused venomously.

Babala felt Huru tense and sensed his rising anger. 'And what if I am?' he asked dangerously, staring at the guard, challenging him. Nothing more was said, only the gusting night wind disturbing the tense silence, the cloaks they wore, and Babala's hair, silvery in the moonlight.

The guard stood up to Huru, but gradually his bravado and his erection waned as he clearly recognised the folly of challenging such a powerful figure. The pike lowered. Huru helped it on its way with a backhand swipe, and Babala sighed with relief as the deadly tip clattered on the ground at her feet.

'Very well, Huru,' said the guard, 'I have no argument with you, and no whore is worth spilling blood over. Take her to the crag.' He cast an evil eye at Babala. 'And good riddance to the troublesome bitch.'

Babala and her giant guardian hurried on, the delay putting the fear of pursuit into them. Slowly they made their way down the steep side of the cliff, testing each foothold carefully before searching for the next.

'I know a cave ahead where we can hide until morning,' Huru said, and Babala shuddered in his arms. 'Is something wrong, little one?' he asked, looking down into her eyes.

'There was another cave to which I was taken,' she said, and told him about the palace guards and how she came to be Maxim's slave.

Huru hugged her to him. 'Nothing like that will happen to you in this cave,' he told her. 'It is somewhere I go to be alone - to think. You will be safe there. I will protect you.'

The chill of the night bit deep into Babala's bones, and had it not been for Huru's arm around her she would surely have frozen to death. At the foot of the cliff, as the ground levelled off and they walked on into the night, putting distance between them and the foreboding castle of the Slavemaster and his vicious wife, Babala was suddenly overcome with fatigue and her legs collapsed beneath her. Huru's arm held her easily, and he picked her up and cradled her as her head lolled against his chest and her eyes closed, despite her valiant attempts to stay awake and not be a burden to her new and trusted protector...

Babala awoke and looked up into Huru's kindly eyes, but there was something seriously wrong.

His wrists and ankles were tied with ropes and he was slung excruciatingly, his arms and legs twisted backwards, to the ceiling of the cave! With a shriek of bewilderment and fear she sat up and cast her wide eyes around the dark and crude shelter, and saw shadows huddling in the darkness and heard whispering voices.

'She's awake,' said one.

'And so beautiful,' said another.

Gradually the shadows took on more substance and Babala gasped and drew back at what she saw. There were seven or eight men, all of them short, all of them repulsive, their legs bowed.

'H-how...?' began Babala, slowly backing away on her bottom. 'How did they overpower you, Huru?'

'Maxim must have put out a warning of our flight.' Huru's voice was strained with pain. 'They lay in wait for me.'

'You, be quiet!' ordered one of the grotesque men, and he pushed Huru's knees, setting him swinging and the ropes creaking. 'She is ours now, to do with as we please.'

'Yes,' said another, 'and we shall use her well.' He thrust his groin out in a lewd manner, swinging his gnarled cock from side to side.

'Tie her down,' said the leader, and several bustled about the cave to gather stakes and tools.

'Th-there is no need,' Huru gasped, his face contorted against the pain of the pull on his arms and shoulders and legs. 'She is trained to please and she will not try to escape.'

'All females run from us,' said the leader, and he gave the signal that Babala should be spread-eagled on the straw that had been her bed and tied to stakes that were hammered into the cave floor at her ankles and above her head.

Despite her desperate struggles and curses this was done with relative ease, and Babala felt totally at the foul group's mercy. She looked up to Huru for comfort, and he smiled reassuringly through his grimace of pain.

'She is lovely,' slavered one, his eyes bulging.

'Hm,' murmured another. 'It's as though she offers herself to us willingly.'

Babala closed her eyes in a futile attempt to hide her shame, but at the same time, secretly, she was proud of her body - proud that she was so fully trained to please others. She felt fingers twisting in her golden hair, fumbling with her breasts and plucking her nipples, and probing inquisitively at her sex lips. They mauled her flesh - her face, her arms, her flat tummy and her legs.

The leader rubbed his cock, pulling back the foreskin to bare the shining globe, slick with issue. It was large, looking out of proportion to his wizened frame.

Babala cringed and held her breath as she felt the warmth and wetness of a tongue rasping her sex. Unable to writhe away from the teasing tongue because of her bonds, she could only lie there and endure the attention, feel the tongue easing between her slick lips and stabbing at the sensitive bud of her clitoris. She was helpless in the tight bindings wrapped around her wrists and ankles; but did she really want to squirm away from the delicious sensations the tongue and hands were giving her? Her molesters were ugly and misshapen, but a familiar heat grew in the pit of her belly and the shameful desire to offer herself fully to her captors was intense.

The leader of the vulgar group gripped Babala's thighs and hunched down between the straddled limbs, and despite her overriding repugnance, a deliciously wanton feeling grew within her and she could feel her creamy sap melded with the man's spittle and seeping over her bottom cheeks. Her clitty felt greatly engorged under his fumbling attentions - tight, as if it would burst with pleasure, and she could not help but mew with ecstasy despite the discomfort of the bindings that pinned her arms and legs outstretched.

The coarse huddle of dirty men murmured and slobbered, and daring to peer from beneath lowered eyelids, Babala saw them looming over her, groping her flesh, their cocks bloated and straining for release.

She heard Huru bellow his rage, as if in great pain, and managed to catch sight of him straining at the thick ropes that held him suspended to the ceiling of the cave, and then the leader shuffled between her thighs, fumbling to position his cock at her entrance.

The others became even more intense, panting and grunting, urging their comrade on, and she could smell their growing excitement, feel the heat of their bodies. The leader sank into her and his cock was long and thick, filling her with one long thrust. Such was his need that he scarcely had time to grind into her more than three or four times before she heard him grunt his pleasure and felt him come deep inside her trussed body.

He slumped to the side, his hairy form drenched with sweat, his chest heaving as he filled his lungs.

'It's my turn,' another demanded eagerly, giving his leader a shove to clear the way and then throwing himself upon her helpless body as he jabbed at her with his bursting erection. 'You'll not escape so lightly this time,' he grunted. 'This time it will be slower, will last longer...' He eased his hands beneath Babala's buttocks and began to thrust with his scrawny hips while he suckled and drooled on her nipples, and despite his confident words he soon stiffened and groaned and Babala felt him coming too as a cock-head nudged against her lips, demanding entry to the warm delights of her mouth.

From then on Babala's mind blurred, until eventually her weary captors slunk away to the shadows in corners and crevices of the cave, and she could hear their muffled breathing and wheezing as they settled down to sleep.

She must have drifted into a troubled doze herself, because after what seemed like mere minutes Huru woke her. He knelt at her side, his comfortingly large hands fumbling with the knots of the ropes that held her spread-eagled on the straw on the cave floor.

'They're all asleep,' he whispered. 'We must leave here quickly.'

'But, how did you - ?'

'Escape?' Huru grinned and showed her his wrists, raw where the ropes had cut into his flesh. 'Brute strength; it comes in handy sometimes.'

'Oh, poor Huru,' said Babala, taking first one hand and then the other and gently kissing the sore wounds.

'Enough - we must go,' he whispered urgently. 'Before these little fiends wake up. Having taken their pleasure of you they will make no bones about carrying out Maxim's orders.'

'Maxim's orders?'

'They have orders to kill you,' he said, sweeping Babala up into his arms and stooping to make his way from the oppressive dungeon of a cave. 'And then me.'

Shivering with fear and cold Babala felt a little better to be again snuggled close to the big man's chest. 'Where shall we go now?' she asked timorously. There seemed to be nowhere safe for them.

'You need rest,' said Huru. 'There is a woodcutter's hut I know deep in the forest. We'll get some rest there.'

Soon they reached the forest, which was forebodingly dark and quiet despite the creeping dawn. Not even the birds were waking, but eventually they reached a tiny clearing and there was a small hut made of logs, roughly cut. Grey smoke trailed up lazily from a stone chimney.

The door opened almost immediately upon Huru's knock. The man who opened it looked genial and kindly enough, but Babala noticed how his eyes glinted as he drank in her beauty.

'Huru,' he greeted, his unsettling eyes not leaving her. 'You've been given leave from the castle? About time - come in.' He stood aside to allow Huru and his precious companion entrance, licking his lips with intent as she was brushed past him.

'No leave, Maro,' Huru said ruefully. 'I left and brought this angel with me.'

'Oh?' said Maro, looking uneasy about the newcomer's announcement. 'A whore, is she? From Maxim's seraglio?'

'Not a whore, no,' Huru insisted firmly. 'As I said, she is an angel. A gentle girl who has been used badly at the castle, but who was still prepared to show me great kindness.'

He laid her upon the truckle bed that huddled in the corner of the single room, and so exhausted was she that almost immediately her eyes closed again and she drifted into sleep.

It was full daylight when Babala awoke, and she sat up with a start when she remembered where she was and realised she was alone with the woodcutter. 'W-where is Huru?' she asked nervously.

'I've sent him to cut some wood,' said the man, 'as payment, you might say, for hiding you two runaways.' He grinned at her and the expression made Babala shiver under the animal skins that warmed her. He was not old, but neither was he young, and the light from the opening that served as a tiny window shone on his bald head.

'I promised him that I would take care of you, my pretty.' He reached out and laid a rough hand on her bare shoulder, and began to stroke her in a familiar manner that made her cringe.

But she did not pull away, for she had been well trained and she knew exactly what the man wanted. 'I'm... I'm a little sore, sir,' she whispered honestly, not wanting to offend Huru's friend, 'from what I've had to endure these past days.'

Maro stroked a hand over his large forehead, which glistened with sweat although the little room was not overly hot. 'So I understand,' he said with a nod, his voice becoming thick with lust, 'but you have these...' and he traced the tip of a grimy finger suggestively around the parted margins of her moist lips, inducing a familiar knot of warmth in her tummy despite her dislike of him.

Maro fed the finger suggestively into her mouth, pumped it crudely in and out a few times, ginning lecherously, then slowly withdrew it from her lips and held it up, turning it this way and that to inspect the sheen of moisture that now coated it. 'And I've noticed you have a very nice bottom, too,' he said huskily, and threw back her fur coverings, smiling lustfully at her nakedness. 'So why don't you roll over like the good girl Huru says you are and let me look at your dear bottom cheeks again? Don't you think it would be a nice idea to show me a little gratitude for risking the wrath of Maxim by giving you shelter?'

'Well... I...' Put like that, how could Babala refuse the man? So she turned onto her front.

'Oh yes,' Maro said quietly, almost to himself, his feverish eyes absorbing her lithe beauty, 'such a lovely girl... such a pretty bottom.' And then he reached out a little hesitantly, as though scared she might suddenly disappear, and smoothed a calloused hand over the luscious contours of her buttocks. 'And...' his voice, thick with carnal longing, caught in his throat, '...and do you like your little rear hole to be breached, my pretty?'

Babala felt stubby fingers press into the valley between her buttocks, and one in particular probe at her hidden anus.

'Ah, I see that you do,' Maro breathed huskily, seeing and feeling the minute roll of her hips, and the finger pressed inquisitively against the tightness of the wrinkled bud. 'And you've been such a naughty girl, haven't you, my pretty?'

'I have?' Babala said innocently, unable to think why.

'Oh yes,' the man said, his eyes fixed obsessively to the soft mounds of her buttocks, his palm moulding the nearest one and his finger continuing to gently probe and test the elasticity of her rear hole, 'very naughty. By coming to my home you risk bringing danger to me. For that I think you need to be punished, don't you?'

'I don't know, sir.' Babala was confused - confused by all that had happened to her in recent days and confused by the wicked sensations his crude attentions were coaxing from her.

'Oh, I do, my pretty,' he croaked. 'And you do need to be punished, believe me...' and then his expression grew suddenly more intense, his hand lifted from her bottom, hovered above her, she tensed, awaiting the inevitable, and then the hand swept down and cracked upon her unguarded globes, making her shriek and the beaten flesh quiver.

'Ouch! Why did you ah - !' the question was wrenched from her lips as his hand struck again, and then the brute set about spanking her with a steady, relentless rhythm and force. Babala instinctively tried to roll away from the onslaught, but she was wedged against the wall with nowhere to go.

'Stay still and accept your punishment, my pretty,' he said hoarsely, the effort of spanking her increasing the beads of sweat on his forehead and making him blink the salt from his eyes. But he was undeterred, focussed totally on the perfect quivering buttocks of the writhing beauty, his hand striking with precise uniformity.

'*Please*...!' Babala shrieked, despite the secret excitement simmering in the pit of her stomach, 'why are you being so spiteful?'

'Because you deserve it,' he said flatly, his eyes glued to the rapidly reddening target of mouth-watering flesh. 'And because you enjoy being spanked, my pretty, do you not?'

He smacked her again and again, and Babala knew it was futile to try to writhe away from the labour-hardened hand. She buried her face in the stale-smelling blanket on the cot, and could protest no more; so intense was her humiliation - and her growing excitement. Then a wave of shamefully submissive bliss washed over her, and she even lifted her bottom a little higher to meet the downward sweep of the man's rough palm.

Maro noticed, of course, and slapped harder, first on one gorgeous cheek and then the other, as she began to move her bottom and hips in a rhythmic and encouraging motion. 'Ah, I know what you want,' he growled.

Babala felt the cot sink a little and heard it creak, and looking up she found him kneeling over her, his bloated cock bared and thrusting from the dark patch of his humid groin at her flushed face.

'Suck it, my pretty,' he grunted. 'Show me your gratitude for giving you shelter. Suck it!'

Babala, knowing it was pointless to deny the man, rested on one elbow, took the throbbing cock between her fingers and touched the globe to her lips. With the very tip of her tongue she probed into the pore and tasted the salty bitterness of the man. She heard him sigh gutturally and began to draw the stubby organ into her mouth, very slowly, feeling the smooth skin and the bloated veins which wound around its girth.

Her bottom still smarted from the spanking, but she diligently caressed his cock with her lips and tongue, pumping with her small fist, and he thrust his groin harder against her face, burying her nose and lips in his course pubic thatch. She heard him growl his pleasure, grunting crude humiliating words, which secretly excited her.

'Yesss... suck my cock, you lovely little harlot,' he croaked, but in her submissive mood she did not mind the insults; for some reason, probably because of her training by the Taskmaster, she wanted to please Maro.

'Ahh!' he groaned, and she felt his cock pulse mightily in her mouth. He thrust even harder against her face and the tip of his turgid length throbbed deep on her tongue, butting into her throat, almost making her gag, but she steeled herself and tried to relax. Maro gripped her head, his strong fingers like iron in her hair, clamping her tight to his groin and holding her still as he shuddered and came, his cock buried in her mouth to the root and his spunk bitter as it discharged down her throat.

His chin slumped to his chest and he closed his eyes, wheezing heavily, and the crush on her head gradually eased. He remained kneeling like that for long moments, the dank little room still and quiet except for his heavy breathing, which slowly returned to a steadier rhythm. Babala felt his flesh softening and the stretch of her lips lessening, and waited patiently until he was ready to slump away from her and flop back onto his creaky chair, relaxed and replete, his sturdy arms dangling by his side, his eyes closed and a faint smile on his fat lips as if he was dozing and enjoying a pleasurable daydream.

'Sir?' she whispered. 'Maro? Do you sleep?'

He frowned and grunted, his eyes still shut. 'What do you want?' His tunic was still above his waist and his shrivelled cock was resting on one of his parted thighs.

'Are you pleased with me?' she asked quietly, not wanting to disturb the man too much and risk incurring the foul temper she sensed he possessed. 'Are you pleased with the way I thanked you for your generosity in giving us shelter?'

'What?' he said gruffly, opening one beady eye. 'What's it to you if I am or if I'm not?' His penis twitched on his thigh. 'You're just a wench who should know when to please a man and when to hold her tongue.' His other eye opened and his gaze crawled over the shapely contours of her body, finally coming to rest on the lovely up-swell of her rosy buttocks, and he licked his lips as his cock twitched again and began to thicken with intent. Babala's eyes were drawn to it as it lifted clear of his hairy thigh and bobbed in the air, pointing at her, and he sniggered as he enjoyed the questioning look of surprise on her face.

'Aye,' he grunted, 'have you ever known such a potent man?'

Babala had, particularly the Taskmaster, but she felt it wise not to say so. 'No sir,' she whispered respectfully.

Maro raised his bulk and reached for her bottom, hunched over her delicious prostrate form. Thick fingers prised her buttocks apart and searched for the tight little orifice. He pressed, and the tip of a finger eased past the determined muscle and popped just inside. Babala moaned, for this rude intrusion only served to renew her simmering excitement.

The finger sank deeper and began to dip in and out of her pulsing rear passage.

'My,' he wheezed, 'but you are a tempting, naughty little morsel...' The finger eased from her rose-hole and the slaps began again, making Babala gasp and her bottom quiver with each blow. 'You deserve to be punished severely,' he hissed hoarsely, as tears filled her eyes and she began to sob with humiliation and frustration, wanting to huddle away from the man yet secretly yearning for more.

Eventually the onslaught slowed and Maro began to stroke her bottom, his mood changing once more. 'You have aroused me again,' he said, somewhat unnecessarily, for the pulsing evidence sprouted from his groin for Babala to see. 'And your wicked bottom beckons for me to sink my manhood into its tightness.' Once more he touched the snug pleats of her anus, pressing and teasing until the hole gave under the pressure and a digit entered the dark, warm place, making her sigh and instinctively raise the soft hillocks of her bottom to his teasing.

The cot creaked as he clambered in ungainly fashion onto it, and she felt the strength of his thighs against the backs of hers as he easily positioned her just as he wanted. Then she felt the thickness of his slippery globe nudging between her buttocks, using his own issue to lubricate the secret entrance, and she could not help but bear up and back against him.

'That's good...' he croaked, his voice thick with arousal, and then Babala stiffened and her forehead lolled down onto the musty blanket as he took his weight on his straightened arms and dropped his hips, impaling her with one easy thrust and pinning her to the cot. Babala groaned, part in discomfort and part in delight. His cock stretched her and pulsed within the tight confines of her bottom.

'How do you like that, my pretty?' he whispered hoarsely in her ear. 'Do I feel huge inside you?'

'Y-yes sir,' she sighed into the blanket. 'Yes sir, you feel very big.'

'Does it hurt?'

'N-no sir... I don't think so...'

'Does it feel good?'

'Yes sir,' she whispered honestly, 'it does feel good.'

Maro started to move, sweating heavily from the exquisite exertions, but then the crack of a fallen branch made him stop and look up at the door, holding his breath and listening intently, wanting to concentrate on the delicious girl who was gently rolling her smooth hips beneath him, her tight rectum milking his cock, but his overriding instinct to sense any possibility of danger coming to the fore.

Heavy feet stamped, as though kicking mud from the soles of boots. 'Maro,' Huru called from the other side of the door. 'I've collected enough wood to sustain a hundred fires for the winter.'

Babala heard him now too, and froze beneath the weight of the sweating man. The door opened and Huru filled the entrance, from where he stopped and stared at the two on the cot. 'What... what are you doing to my angel?' he said simply, but the anger was evident in his tone.

Maro did not move, but relaxed again now that the threat of being caught with the girl by a patrol from the castle had passed. 'Nothing,' he said, a mocking grin on his coarse features. 'Just keeping her company, that's all. Now leave us alone, Huru, so I can finish what I've started,' and he turned his attention back to Babala, lifted his hips and then stabbed his cock down to plug her bottom completely, making her whimper and the cot creak.

'Release her.'

Beneath the straining man Babala looked up at Huru with wide appealing eyes, and could see he was trying to control his temper. But Maro ignored the man at the door, his attention directed solely on the delights of the delicious girl sandwiched between him and the cot, and how wonderful her snug bottom felt as it cosseted his rampant cock.

'Let her go,' Huru said.

'Ha, that might be difficult,' Maro sneered between rhythmic grunts. 'Now go away Huru and leave me in peace to enjoy her properly.'

With two great strides Huru was across the dingy room and he grabbed Maro's shoulders. 'I told you to let her go!' he roared, and pulled his adversary up from the cot, savagely interrupting his onslaught upon Babala's bottom.

'What are you doing?' Maro challenged, with an air of dangerous calm. 'I was enjoying myself there.' He sneered. 'And so was she, believe me...' and then from nowhere there was a flash of metal in the gloom and he held a knife, pointed threateningly at Huru's throat. 'Now, I suggest you do as I say and leave the two of us alone,' he hissed. 'I've some unfinished business with the little whore.'

Babala scrabbled up and sat with her legs folded beneath her, cringing back against the damp wall, holding the furs up around her nakedness. 'Stop it, both of you,' she pleaded.

'Don't call her that,' said Huru, ignoring her attempt to intervene.

Maro sniggered. 'What, whore?' he goaded. 'And why shouldn't I? For that's what she is. And she knows how to use those pretty lips to please a man, that is for sure. And as for her arse...'

Babala knew something awful was about to happen, and she feared for Huru. 'Please, stop this,' she begged. 'Both of you.'

'Be quiet, whore,' growled Maro.

'I told you; don't call her that,' Huru repeated.

'And what will you do if I - '

Huru's great fist swung in a vicious and surprisingly swift arc and clubbed Maro on the side of the head before he had a chance to counter with the knife, instantly silencing the man's mocking tones and knocking him sideways. Huru's rage was up, so he grabbed a thick bough from the log basket beside the fire.

'Huru, no!' shrieked Babala, but he brought it down anyway and cracked it against Maro's temple, knocking him to his knees. The bough lifted, the knife flashed dangerously in the dim light, but the wood swept down again knocking the woodcutter unconscious, dropping him heavily face down on the floor.

'I am sorry, little one,' Huru said, dropping the bough and turning quickly to Babala. 'I should never have left you alone with him. I thought he could be trusted.'

Babala shook her head. 'It doesn't matter,' she said sadly. 'Maro was no different to all the others, and it is not all bad. Sometimes I like it. I was taught to like it by the Taskmaster. He said I was born to be enjoyed by men.'

Huru winced and staggered a little, and with a gasp of shock Babala noticed his calf was bleeding from a deep gash in the muscle. Maro's desperate lunge with the knife had caught him. 'You're hurt,' she said, easing her aching body up from the rickety cot. 'Let me tend the wound. I'll get some clean water from the well.'

'It is nothing,' said Huru, putting a hand on her arm to stop her. 'We must leave quickly before Maro recovers and sends word for Maxim's guards to hunt us down like dogs. He is a vengeful man when crossed,' he looked down at the unconscious heap on the floor, 'and I think our friendship is at an end.'

'But you can't go with your leg bleeding like that,' Babala protested, looking round for something to stem the flow.

'No, we must not waste time,' Huru insisted, sounding impatient as he wrapped Babala in a large animal pelt. 'We must go, and we must go *now*.' He picked her up and hurried out of the gloomy hut.

After only a short distance into the forest Huru was limping badly, but he would not hear of them stopping, even for a moment to rest.

'Have you any idea what Maxim's men will do to you if they catch us?' he warned, and hurried on as quickly as his wound would allow.

As Babala looked back she saw the trail Huru was leaving, dark specks of blood on the carpet of fallen leaves, and she shivered despite the wrapping of fur about her.

The forest was almost silent, even the birds had stopped their singing. The only sounds were the slightly uneven stride of Huru's pounding feet and the brush of the vegetation as he stomped through it. His arms held her closely to his chest.

'Not too much further now,' Huru panted, his pace not letting up despite it being some hours since they had fled the hut. 'Not long now before we reach the far edge of the forest, and then we'll be in the sloping pasture and the town will be below us. Not long.'

His words soothed Babala and she at last began to relax, and Huru's steady jogging was like a rocking cradle, but no sooner had she begun to feel safe than she heard excited shouts disturbing the peace of the forest behind them. There were dogs, too - large and ferocious, judging by the sounds of their barks. Huru stopped and looked back, his eyes narrowed as he stared through the gloom beneath the forest canopy. He was limping badly now and the bleeding had not staunched.

'They're near!' someone shouted. 'The dogs are getting excited!'

'It's the blood they can smell,' said Huru, as much to himself as to Babala. 'I've led them to you. I'm sorry.' He leaned back against an oak tree and Babala was frightened as she looked at his drained face. He was a horrible pale colour and seemed to have given up. They were in a small clearing and Huru was too weary to outrun their pursuers, and then a commotion made her look back and there were the hunters, their fierce dogs straining at their leashes, fangs bared and drool dripping from their jowls.

'We've got them, lads!' one of the men shouted, raising a hand and waving more of them over to where he stood. 'We've got them! The woodcutter was right!'

Huru set Babala on her feet and pulled the animal skin close about her. 'Be brave, little one,' he said, 'as I know you always are. And whatever you do, do not let them break your spirit.'

Babala began to weep, not for herself but for Huru, who had been such a brave and loyal companion since they left the castle. The hunters stalked around the pair, careful not to get too close to Huru, who could still be dangerous. The growling dogs strained forward, up on their hind legs, pulling on their leashes.

Then the leader beckoned Babala to him, and Huru resignedly let her go. The man roughly turned her round, stripped the animal skin from her and cast it to the ground, where the snarling dogs pounced on it, tearing and shredding with their fangs.

Once again Babala was naked and vulnerable, so she stood very still, waiting for whatever the hunters would do next. They looked her up and down with lustful stares, twisted her round and inspected her bottom that still bore the inflamed marks from Maro's beating.

They were burly men, almost as large as Huru, thick shouldered with muscular arms and legs, and dressed in the usual short tunic. They wasted no time in clipping manacles with short chains to Babala's wrists and ankles.

'Don't hurt her,' Huru warned them as he was chained to a tree, but the hunters just laughed and told him to hold his tongue.

'Are you taking us back to the castle?' asked Babala, as a linking chain was fastened from her wrist cuffs to the ankle chains.

The men laughed again. 'Nothing so comfortable,' said one. 'When we've finished with you we're to take you to the town and leave you to the lowlife that lives there.'

'The girl is a beautiful sight, I must admit,' said one. 'I can't imagine why Maxim is suddenly so keen to be rid of her.'

'He's decided she brings too much trouble,' explained another. 'He told us to track her and her halfwit friend down to send out a clear message to anyone else who might harbour thoughts of fleeing the castle without permission. But he doesn't want her taken back.' The man leered, and then added ominously, 'He said we can do with her as we please.'

Then, while Huru looked on hopelessly, Babala was laid on the damp ground and engulfed by the avaricious men.

Her lips were prised open and an erection plugged her mouth. Her thighs were parted and another rigid column penetrated her. Countless hands mauled, and pinched and slapped. Without either of the erections disengaging or even interrupting their rhythmic pumping, she was rolled onto her side and another shaft stabbed into her bottom while hands pulled her buttocks apart.

As the day wore on each of the men took their share of their unresisting captive more than once, with Huru having to witness their enjoyment and her shame.

Then, when the men were utterly sated, an exhausted Babala was carried, still in chains, to the edge of the forest and down to the outskirts of the town.

Chapter 11

The Lady Fazath was dressed as a noblewoman, in a rich velvet gown cut low at her breasts, revealing her inviting cleavage, and a cloak that swirled from her shoulders and fell heavily to her feet. 'But we don't even know that she is in this wretched little town,' she complained.

'No, we don't,' agreed the Taskmaster. He also wore clothes that classed him as a gentleman. It was necessary, noticed Fazath, for him to make many adjustments at his crotch, for he was more used to the simple loincloth that lightly covered his cock but allowed it freedom. 'But I'd be willing to guess that she has been taken into one of the bordellos around here, and there are plenty of them.'

'We don't know that,' said Fazath, lifting her skirts to keep them from dragging in the rotting garbage strewn about the street. 'I saw her taken away by the Slavemaster.'

'And who knows what that harridan of a wife of his would make of that,' said the Taskmaster. 'No, we'll search the bordellos. If the rumours of her recapture after her flight from the castle are true, that's where she'll be, mark my words, being used by anyone who can pay a price.'

Lady Fazath shuddered. 'Poor girl.'

A tavern door was open and the noise of raucous revelry drifted out onto the street, and Fazath had to quickly dodge a man who staggered drunkenly from the doorway - but she was too late. 'They wouldn't let me...' he slurred sorrowfully, stumbling to his knees and grabbing the hem of her gown. 'They wouldn't let me...'

'Get away from me!' she hissed venomously, trying to tug the velvet from the clutch of his filthy hands.

'Wait,' said the Taskmaster, frowning at Fazath. He bent down and smiled at the pitiful man. 'Wouldn't let you what?' he asked.

'There's a new girl,' said the drunk, still pulling at the hem of Fazath's gown while she tugged in the opposite direction. 'A new girl in the seraglio upstairs. A beauty, by all accounts, and they wouldn't let me see her, let alone spend some time with her.'

'It's her,' said the Taskmaster, straightening up. 'I'm sure it's Babala.'

'Let go!' Lady Fazath pulled on the velvet one last time and the gown ripped, baring her legs and bottom. 'You wretched man!' she screamed, and attempted to wrap the cloak around her, but the Taskmaster stayed her hand.

'Don't.' He stood back and stared at her slender bare hips and legs.

'Don't?' Lady Fazath tried once more to cover herself, as much from the lewd stare of the drunk at her feet as from the Taskmaster and the occasional passer-by.

'You look so attractive like that,' he explained. 'Come along.' He grabbed her hand and pulled her through the open tavern door.

'What are you doing?' Lady Fazath again tried to wrap her cloak close about her, but the Taskmaster swung her round and draped her over a table, face down between the tankards and caring nothing for the chill of the spilled ale which cooled her breasts and tummy. He lifted the cloak and fully bared her bottom.

Fazath squealed as her buttocks were suddenly on fire under the weight of the Taskmaster's hand, and the tavern was instantly silent at the sound of flesh smacking flesh.

'I believe you're looking for girls to service your bordello,' he said to the slob behind the counter, and then pulled Fazath to her feet.

'Girls, yes,' said the innkeeper, 'but that one should have been retired long ago.'

There was a burst of sniggers and coarse remarks from the drunken customers and serving wenches alike.

'But she's a handsome woman,' said the Taskmaster, opening Fazath's mouth to show the healthy state of her teeth.

Inwardly she fumed. This was what the wretch had planned all along, she told herself. It was all an elaborate plan - to use her to find Babala by putting her, Fazath, to work in every bordello in the town.

'Turn round, my dear,' said the Taskmaster. 'And over the table again.'

'Don't you dare slap me,' she hissed.

'Do you want to find Babala?' he asked under his breath. 'Then do as you're told.' He flashed a winning smile at the innkeeper. 'A nice tight arse, you see?' he said, pressing a finger into Fazath's rosebud, much to her intense humiliation. 'Turn over and open your legs,' he ordered her.

The Lady Fazath peered around the smoky bar and found herself gazing into the interested brown eyes of one of the wenches. So long as she kept that pretty image in her head she would not feel so humiliated and, one never knew, perhaps she and the wench might have some fun together in one of the upstairs rooms. So obediently, she lay on her back with her knees parted.

'See how lithe and firm she is,' said the Taskmaster. 'Nothing sags here. All is toned and fresh'

'And ripe!' bawled the innkeeper.

The Taskmaster ignored the remark while Fazath again fumed at being so humiliatingly displayed before the whole drunken rabble. She felt her sex lips being spread by the Taskmaster's fingers, felt him tap the tip of her nubbin to show how erect it was, and felt him draw back the little hood to completely expose the sensitive part. 'As pink and healthy as a younger woman's,' he remarked.

From the corner of her eye Fazath noticed the serving wench move to the front of the crowd and lick her lips as she stared between her open thighs. A smile lifted the corner of the girl's mouth and she parted her lips to enable a finger to be placed, in a very obviously lewd gesture, between them. Fazath returned the smile, and she could almost ignore the lecherous mob.

'What do you say?' coaxed the Taskmaster. 'Will you take her on in your bordello?'

'I'm not sure,' said the innkeeper. 'Can she do tricks?'

'What kind of tricks?' The Taskmaster frowned at the question. He was becoming impatient, for Fazath was not the only one who had seen the pretty serving wench. His cock was swollen in the tight confines of his hose and he was forced to adjust its mighty coil to a more comfortable position.

'Oh, I don't know,' said the innkeeper. He was impatient too. This wasn't selling any ale, nor was he collecting revenue from the bordello upstairs. 'Let's see how flexible her entrances are,' he said.

'What are you doing?' Fazath snapped.

'Lift your bottom,' said the innkeeper, ignoring the question, 'and keep your legs apart. Let us see just what you can take.'

The Lady Fazath, quite appalled by the rude man, fixed her gaze on the serving wench, and the thought of the plump but firm young body lying quite naked under hers as she lapped at a juicy cunny took all thoughts of humiliation from her mind.

She felt fingers spreading her bottom cheeks to reveal the tight bud of her anus, but even this did not upset her as she thought of full young breasts being cradled in her hands as she sucked first upon one taut nipple and then another.

Something pressed into her bottom - a stubby finger, but it wasn't an unpleasant sensation.

'Uh-huh,' the innkeeper mused thoughtfully, like a doctor examining his patient. Then he fingered the creamy opening of her cunny, and eased two fingers deep inside, his rough palm agitating her clitoris. Fazath's sex gently convulsed around the invading digits with secret excitement, as she let her fantasies dwell on the serving wench and imagined spanking the little minx's bottom, which she was sure was as pale as driven snow and just as smooth.

'Excellent!' exclaimed the innkeeper. 'The woman has good strength in her cunt muscles after all.'

'Of course I do!' Fazath protested indignantly, raising herself on her elbows. 'I have always kept myself in excellent condition.' She gave the serving wench a meaningful look and the girl bowed her head in a gesture of delightful submission. Oh, she was going to have such fun with that one!

'Shhh!' warned the Taskmaster, pushing her flat upon the table again, and then turning to the innkeeper. 'Perhaps you would like to proceed?' he invited.

'Hm,' the innkeeper nodded. He caressed the open outer lips, spreading them until all huddled near enough could see the prominence of her erect clitty.

'Be my guest,' encouraged the Taskmaster, and Fazath gave him a furious glare as the innkeeper started to strum her succulent and sensitive flesh. The Taskmaster patted her shoulder in a comforting, encouraging gesture. 'You're doing well,' he said quietly.

Her eyes were again drawn to the serving wench. How she wished those pretty lips were petting her clitty instead of the crude fumbling fingers of the innkeeper. How she wished that dear little tongue could tease her anus...

So deep in these lewd thoughts was she that at first she did not recognise a tongue lapping at her tortured clitty. It was only when the first waves of pleasure warmed her trim belly and began to make her juices flow more copiously that she realised a customer had sunk down between her straddled legs and was lapping busily at her, encouraged by the drunken rabble.

'Oh, stop him,' she moaned, trying to squirm away from the insidious tongue.

'But why, my dear?' asked the Taskmaster. 'You know how you love an active tongue seeking out all the delicate morsels of your cunny.' He continued stroking her shoulder.

'But, please, not a man...' She sighed, but despite her protests the sensations were turning her on incredibly. 'I wouldn't mind you, if it has to be a man,' she confessed, 'but... but, I really want *her*...' and as a beautiful orgasm wracked her body and the rabble cheered and slopped ale onto the dirty floor from their mugs she managed to point with a trembling finger at the delicious serving wench who still stood, hands clasped meekly together and eyes lowered.

'I'll take her!' the innkeeper announced decisively.

'Good,' said the Taskmaster. 'I knew you were a shrewd man of taste the minute I set eyes on you. Come along,' he said to Fazath, 'upstairs with you.'

The Lady Fazath, looking much dishevelled, slipped from the ale-soaked table with shaky legs. The Taskmaster supported her, and began to lead her to the rickety wooden stairs that led to the upper floor.

'And where do you think you're going?' asked the innkeeper.

'To escort her to your chambers,' answered the Taskmaster.

The innkeeper shook his head decisively. 'No pimps allowed.'

'Pimp? I am no pimp.'

'Ruth,' the innkeeper beckoned to the cute serving wench, ignoring the Taskmaster's defence of himself. 'Take our new whore to the bedchambers. And wash her ready for the real paying customers.' He waved a hand disparagingly at the ale drinkers, who, now that the excitement was over, had returned to the business of supping from their tankards.

With a face like thunder the Taskmaster agreed to leave. 'But I don't suppose you will refuse a customer when I return,' he said sarcastically as he stomped through the tavern doors.

The girl, Ruth, at the Lady Fazath's side, smelled intoxicatingly alluring. Her firm breasts threatened to spill from her bodice, pushed up and squeezed together as they were by the tightly laced stomacher. Her long skirt, although stained by ale and food, was entrancing, tucked up at one side to bare a firm thigh so that the hem did not drag in the puddles, grime and sawdust.

'Why does the innkeeper not use you in his bordello?' asked Fazath.

'Because I am his daughter, ma'am,' said Ruth, 'and a virgin.'

'A virgin,' sighed Fazath, utterly smitten. 'A virgin - how delightful.' Her thoughts drifted to beneath Ruth's skirts, between her delicious thighs and to her dear little quim, untouched by another's hand. Babala would have been equally pure had not the Taskmaster got to her first. Would the innkeeper find out if she, Fazath, indulged in some fun with his daughter?

'My father wants me to marry well,' said Ruth, her pretty head bowed modestly, 'and he says that no man will take me for a wife if my maidenhead is broken.'

'Quite right, my dear,' Fazath agreed sombrely, but her voice was husky with lust, imagining the delicious secrets beneath Ruth's skirts: the full, unblemished bottom cheeks, the plump sex lips so gloriously decorated with fiery red curls, for the girl's hair was a tumble of red-gold, and between those plump lips... oh, such delights! Such mouth-watering thoughts made her fair dizzy to think of them.

'In which room are you going to tend me?' she asked, trying to control her mounting excitement. But oh, to have the girl sponging her private parts while she lay back with her legs parted. It was just too enticing to contemplate! If she thought about it for very much longer she would surely orgasm before the girl had even started to ready her.

'In here,' said Ruth, shyly opening one of the heavy oak doors. 'All the chambers are much the same, but this one will serve and we shall not be disturbed.'

This last statement sent a thrill surging through Fazath and made her stomach churn with anticipation. 'That's good,' she murmured. 'I should hate for that to happen.'

Ruth gave Fazath a shy glance; her eyelashes lowered as if the task her father had set made her uncomfortable.

The small room was dimly lit by a few candles, with a four-poster bed at its centre. The girl's scent was like nectar to Fazath as they stood close together. There was a sweetness about it, with a freshness that reminded Fazath of the gardens around the palace of Ellipsis, her old home.

Soon the sweet thing had helped her undress, and standing naked in the bedchamber, despite her wealth of experience in seducing delightful young maidens, Fazath almost trembled with excitement. She was sure the girl's delicious scent would be even more intoxicating if she could be persuaded to undress also.

'Why don't you take off your bodice and skirt, my dear?' Fazath purred seductively. 'You will be so much more comfortable...' and without awaiting a response she began to unlace the girl's stomacher, expecting whispered protests and shy hands to try to prevent her at any moment, but there was nothing; no unfavourable reaction. Once unlaced, allowing Fazath shadowy glimpses of the tempting milky flesh within, the girl stood as still as a statue as the older woman slipped the garment from her.

'Isn't that better?' she cooed, and Ruth nodded shyly as Fazath savoured the way the cascade of red-gold hair tumbled richly over her pale shoulders. Slowly, carefully, Fazath reached out to caress the ripeness of her enticing breasts, but the girl stepped back.

'I must get on with my duties,' she said, and began to pour water from a pitcher into a porcelain bowl. Perfumed steam rose from the water and Fazath, wondering how she would ever keep her hands off the delicious girl, sat on the edge of the bed and parted her thighs. Oh, how she wished the girl would lick her between them with her pretty tongue, but instead she felt the warm softness of a scrap of flannel being wiped, first over her jet-black bush and then between her sex lips, and it was as much as she could do not to moan with pleasure.

She watched avidly as Ruth's pert breasts swayed as she went about her work. Her nipples were taut as though she too was aroused. How she reminded Fazath of Babala! Her hair was a darker red and less golden, but Ruth had that same meekness, that pliant submissiveness that always aroused Fazath.

When her sex was cleansed and patted dry Fazath lay back, heavy-limbed from her excitement, on the bed. She watched Ruth go about her business, tidying the dressing stand with neat precise movements, and the vision made her shudder with delight.

What would Ruth do, she wondered, if she jumped from the bed and grabbed that lovely body, held it in her arms and perhaps gave those lovely buns a sound slapping? She would probably scream, and that could be a problem. She looked around for something, anything she could use as a gag. There were the curtain ties; they were long enough to gag her and tie her wrists.

Unable to resist the alluring beauty any longer, Fazath made her move. Silently she rose and went to the window, and took the ties from their hooks. Sensing movement Ruth turned, and seeing Fazath with the tie she opened her mouth to speak, making it all the easier for the practised woman to push the length between those deliciously soft lips. The rope was wrapped twice around Ruth's pretty face and tied tightly about her wrists, which Fazath pinned behind her back.

There was no resistance, Fazath noticed, as she removed her skirt. Was it that the girl was too shocked by her move, or just exquisitely submissive? She picked Ruth up, cradling her in her arms, and felt the slightest shiver run through her light burden, but at that moment could not discern whether it was a shudder of distaste or delight.

Ruth was placed face down on the brocade cover and Fazath adjusted her tied wrists so that they did not impede her view of those delicious buttocks. Still Ruth did not struggle or make any sign that the treatment was abhorrent to her. She was so like Babala; so submissive, and so sweetly compliant.

'Have you ever been smacked on your bottom?' Fazath asked huskily.

Ruth nodded her head against the soft pillows.

'By your father?'

Again Ruth nodded.

'Why? Because you were naughty?'

She nodded again.

'Poor girl.' Fazath stroked the lovely bottom mounds, admiring their perfection and unblemished beauty. The innkeeper, she decided, must be an expert disciplinarian for the buns were quite unmarked, or perhaps it was some time since her last spanking. She noticed Ruth was wriggling slightly, instinctively. Perhaps she enjoyed being spanked, and was hoping to be spanked now. There was no doubt that some girls did relish being chastised by Fazath's experienced hand.

The dominant woman raised her arm and Ruth watched over her shoulder with wide sparkling eyes. She lifted her bottom and the slap was loud in Fazath's ears, and it was so very arousing. She felt an immediate flush of warmth between her cunny lips and a swelling of her clitty. It was so long since she felt like this. Not since she had lost Babala. She could see the scarlet of her handprint on the background of pouting bottom flesh. It was more than a woman like Fazath could bear not to enhance the feeling again with another flat-palmed slap.

She thought she heard a mew of pleasure, much as Babala used to respond. This only encouraged Fazath to smack harder the third time, and harder still the fourth. Again and again the slaps rained down until the pale flesh was no longer white but scarlet and blotchy, and looking breathtakingly delicious for it.

'I know you are a virgin,' murmured Fazath, leaning over the trembling girl, 'and I would not dream of breaking that precious maidenhead of yours, but what would you say to a tongue between these tender buns.' She illustrated her meaning with a fingertip, drawn between the tight cheeks and allowed to linger at the tiny anus. 'And when I have brought you to a lovely come,' she whispered, 'perhaps we could lie top to tail and you could return the favour?'

The girl was breathing heavily, but Fazath could not discern whether this was from the pleasure she had already experienced from the smacking or that which was to come from the attentions of her finger and tongue. 'Come along now,' she encouraged, 'what do you think?'

Ruth wriggled her bottom as if pressing her sex mound into the soft feather bed to gain pleasure from its folds working their way into her pink virginal pleats.

The bound and gagged girl looked at the seductress over her shoulder, speaking volumes with her pleading eyes.

'Don't worry, your father is busy with his customers,' said Fazath, understanding the unspoken question. 'Does the place between your thighs feel hot and sensitive?' she asked.

The girl nodded again, her flame-red hair cascading over the pillows.

'Then let me ease it,' cajoled Fazath. 'It will be very pleasant for us both. How old are you, my dear?' she added. 'Seventeen... eighteen?'

The girl mewed softly in answer, and Fazath could feel her excitement mounting. 'Eighteen,' she sighed. Babala was a little younger than that when she was first taken to the Taskmaster, she thought.

She lay down between the girl's thighs and could smell her freshness. Playfully, she used her long raven hair to tickle the scalded buttocks. Ruth whimpered behind the gag and lifted her sex pouch to ease Fazath's task.

'Oh, how sweet you are,' murmured the cunning woman. 'A pillow beneath your belly will make this all the easier.' Ruth whimpered again as this was accomplished and tilted her cunny mound to give Fazath full access to her.

As Fazath expected, the girl's sex had the delicious smooth fullness of youth, with the lips already engorged about the erect clitoris. They were pink and flushed with beads of milky sap glittering like pearls on the inner folds.

'Do you ever play with yourself?' Fazath purred, gazing entranced at the succulent sex. 'When alone in bed at night, for example?' She stroked the red-gold curls of the outer lips, feeling their plumpness, and then allowed her fingers to part them fully to give her a full view of the pretty picture.

Ruth, still gagged, could say nothing and Fazath, her own playfulness with the girl making her impatient, slithered up the girl's smooth body until she could feel the heat of her smacked bottom beneath her own sex. 'Tell me the truth now,' Fazath murmured into her ear.

The pretty face was hot from blushing and there was no need for words. It was obvious what the truth was.

'So you do.' Fazath remained where she was, stroking the silkiness of her mound back and forth over Ruth's bottom. 'You seek out your sex bud with those naughty little fingers and rub it back and forth until that glorious feeling comes over you, and afterwards you lie there, waiting for the pleasure to subside and wishing a man would plunge his cock into you...' Fazath felt unreasonably angry at the thought, but knew that her real emotion was envy; envy that she did not have a cock to plunge into the girl, to slide in and out on the creamy lubrication of sap. 'Admit it.' She coaxed harshly. 'Isn't that what you do?' She slid her hands under the slender body and cupped the full breasts to tweak the hardened pink buds.

The gag slipped slightly, the cord wet with Ruth's spittle. 'Yes,' she whispered. 'Yes, I do exactly that.'

'I thought so,' Fazath mused triumphantly, sliding down the girl's body once more. 'A girl who enjoys a spanking on her bare bottom as much as you do must also enjoy the feel of her own fingers within her cunny slit.'

Her fingers probed into the tightness of the bottom cleft, prising it apart to fully reveal the tiny pit of Ruth's anus. It was like a rosebud, tightly folded and pink. Her tongue lapped out and sampled the clean but earthy taste of it. She heard Ruth moan and felt her wriggle, but Fazath had much more to do to the girl before she was finished.

She licked again, this time allowing her tongue to slither from the anus all the way down to the tilted beauty of the girl's cunny. It was soft and fragrant under the touch of her tongue, the flesh as succulent as the juiciest fruit. The girl's musk was strong but intoxicating. Fazath smiled to herself, knowing the reason; she was acutely excited too. Her clitoris was engorged, the sap flowing freely, and it was all Fazath could do to restrain herself from plunging her fingers into Ruth's closed female gateway, but she did, keeping her attentions strictly confined to the delights of the swollen sex folds.

She did, however, press the bud of her anus as she allowed her tongue to slick up and down around her clitty. It was such a delight to feel it pulsing against her tongue, although she knew the girl had not reached her climax yet. She sipped at the juices that were so copious for one so inexperienced. It reminded Fazath of Babala when she first had the opportunity to tongue her. She kissed the juices with soft pecking movements of her pursed lips, and was gratified to hear the delirious mewing of the girl.

At last she homed in on her clitoris, sucking the hardened and throbbing little morsel over and over again. Slowly, drawing the little slip of skin back along the shaft until the tip was quite bare and available, she caressed it with back and forth laps of her tongue, and all the time she kept the gentlest of pressure on her anal bud.

'Oh, this is so glorious,' moaned Ruth. 'Let it go on and on forever. Don't let it stop, *please.*'

The girl had stretched her thighs to their fullest extent and arched her bottom in the air to make her even more fully available to Fazath, and came, her knuckles white as she clutched the bedspread, her orgasm almost violent in its intensity.

When it was over Fazath lay alongside Ruth, kissing the pale sweep of her throat, the trembling softness of her breasts, the delicate swell of her tummy.

'I want you to do it to me again,' Ruth said in a whisper. 'I want you to do it over and over again. It's never like that when I touch myself. It's very nice, but nothing like that.' She kissed Fazath with impulsive innocence. It was a lingering kiss, and she tentatively eased her tongue into Fazath's mouth. Then she drew back and they gazed into each other's eyes. Fazath's were smiling, while Ruth's were bemused.

'Is that what I taste like?' She licked her lips as if savouring her own musk. 'It's nice.' She kissed Fazath again, and then asked, 'Do you taste like that?'

Fazath smiled and nodded, silently encouraging the girl to investigate for herself, and she sighed as Ruth slid down the bed and, with gentle fingers, eased Fazath's unresisting thighs apart. This was what she had planned from the first, and she trembled with excitement as the inquisitive fingers opened her cunny and examined it intimately, parting the folds and fingering the hardness of her clitty.

'I'm not hurting you, am I?' Ruth whispered sweetly.

'Not at all, my dear,' said Fazath, her voice husky with need.

'Can... can I taste you?'

Fazath could feel the gentle waft of the girl's breath, warm and sweet on her open cunny. 'Of course, my sweet,' she said, trying to keep her voice steady, 'but place your legs on either side of my head first.'

'So we can taste each other?' Ruth said excitedly.

'So we can taste each other,' Fazath confirmed. Not since Babala had she known such innocence and yet such enthusiasm for sexual pleasure, and could barely contain herself as the toned thighs straddled her head. She felt their smoothness against each cheek and smelled the girl's musk as her sex nestled over her face. The warm, rich smell was much stronger now after her orgasm, and she felt Ruth's open sex brushing over her lips and sighed as she sucked on the very tip of her vibrant clitty.

And then she felt the girl's inexperienced lips and tongue caress her cunny flesh, felt tentative fingers fumble to part the folds. For all Fazath's years of experience she could not remember feeling such excitement as her fleshpot was kissed. Every sensation was heightened to an ultimate extent as the tongue stroked the length of each trembling leaf. A fingertip patted the naked point of her clitty.

Thoughts of Babala were pushed into the background of Fazath's mind; so heavenly was the taste of this girl, so delicious was the feel of her maiden cunny. What did it matter that she, Fazath, was to be forced to sell her own body to men in an attempt to find Babala? For the moment she had Ruth and her sweet, scarcely touched sex.

She could feel her orgasm rising from the pit of her stomach. Beautiful warmth spread through her whole body. Her limbs felt heavy and wonderfully lethargic, but she was able to open her legs to their fullest extent to give the girl greater access to her fluttering sex. She wanted to scream her delight, but her mouth was full of the innocent's sweet sex flesh. She felt a throb of the hardened clitty and then another and another, until the girl was shuddering on top of her in another strong climax.

'Ruth!' Her name was shouted from along the landing. 'Damn the girl; she's never around when she's needed. Have you finished with the new whore? I have a customer for her.'

Ruth, her pretty face glossed with sex juices, rolled from Fazath. 'Father!' she whispered. 'We have to hurry. If he finds us...' She rubbed her naked bottom ruefully, thinking no doubt of the spanking she would receive if they were found together playing such rude games.

'Hide in the cupboard,' Fazath suggested, and got up to open the roughly hewn door to a hanging wardrobe. 'What does your father like his girls to wear when they receive customers?'

Ruth stepped into the cupboard and pulled a flimsy shift from a hook. 'One of these,' she said, pushing the garment into Fazath's hands. 'Now go quickly - don't let him find me here like this.'

Fazath looked at the shift critically, but slipped it on over her head. It scarcely covered her sex bush and dark curls peeped coyly beneath the hem. 'I might as well be wearing nothing at all,' she grumbled.

'Oh, go quickly!' pleaded Ruth. 'Greet the customer and when father returns to the ale room I shall dress and join him.' She smiled fleetingly. 'Oh, but I have enjoyed myself,' she confided. 'Perhaps I could see you again later tonight... all night.'

'Whenever you wish, my sweet,' Fazath said dreamily. 'Whenever you wish.'

'Ruth! Wherever are you hiding?' The rough voice was angry and Fazath heard heavy footsteps outside the door.

'Quickly now,' she warned, closing the wardrobe door and lifting her chin to face the innkeeper.

'There you are.' Fazath was greeted with a sharp slap on her bare bottom. 'Where's my daughter? Where's Ruth?'

Fazath shrugged. 'I believe you have a customer for me?' she said, avoiding the question.

The innkeeper sniggered. 'Indeed I have. He's an elderly soul, but I thought quite appropriate for you. He won't be too demanding - won't wear you out, if you get my meaning.' He sniggered again, grabbed Fazath's elbow and led her out to a room at the far end of the dimly lit landing.

'I'll have you know,' said Fazath, 'that you're talking to a woman in the prime of life.'

'Is that so?' retorted the innkeeper. 'Then you'll have the strength to work on this customer until he is satisfied, won't you? It'll probably take all night.'

He pushed Fazath through the door and slammed it shut, leaving her alone with her first customer. Her heart sank; she had promised Ruth that they would meet secretly later, but by the look of the wizened old gent standing by the window there would be no later!

All night, thought Fazath; all week might be nearer the truth. He was hunched and held the small of his back as though beset with backache. What hair he had was grizzled and unkempt, and he lent on a walking stick, which was as crooked as he was.

'Well, Fazath,' the old fellow croaked.

'You know my name?'

The old fellow cackled, but then straightened up determinedly, snatched off the hairpiece and threw away the stick as he marched over to her.

'Taskmaster!' she beamed, greatly relieved.

He pulled her close to him, moulding his body to her almost naked one. His lips claimed hers and his tongue probed her mouth. 'A familiar but pleasant aroma,' he remarked with a knowing grin. 'What have you been up to while I risked my welfare to come and rescue you from this hellhole?'

'Risked your welfare?' Fazath could not keep the irony from her voice. 'What about me? You throw me into a brothel to be abused by all and sundry - '

'Never mind that,' he interrupted her, and then lifted the shift and cupped her sex, letting his middle finger slide deep into the soft wetness. No matter how hard she tried Fazath could not escape his grip and was powerless to stop his intimate investigation. 'You've found some girl to service you,' he said. 'Is it Babala? Have you found her?'

'No, it isn't Babala.'

'You say that in a tone of annoyance,' said the Taskmaster, 'as though Babala is no longer important to you. As though she is no longer the girl you risked your life and endured so much for.'

'Of course she's still important to me!'

'But you've found someone who excites you more,' said the Taskmaster. 'That's it, isn't it?'

'She's a virgin,' Fazath confessed breathlessly, 'and so innocent. But she is so sensual too. You would desire her just as much as I do.'

The Taskmaster sat in a chair. 'Then I want her too.'

Fazath shook her head, fearing the worst. 'But you can't; she's a beautiful virgin. Besides, we must see if Babala is here and get away quickly. To linger would be folly.'

'Then she's my kind of girl,' he mused. 'I haven't savoured such innocence since your stupidity and greed tore me away from the Prince's palace. But you are right that we must find Babala, so fetch the girl quickly and bring her to me,' he demanded.

'But she's the innkeeper's daughter,' Fazath protested. 'You'll risk bringing all sorts of trouble upon us if you take her virginity.'

He chuckled. 'Have faith, Fazath. I will not endanger us - I promise. Now bring her to me,' he urged confidently.

'Please, Taskmaster, let's just see if Babala is being employed here, and if she is we get her out, and if she isn't we get out ourselves...'

At that moment there was a tentative tap on the door and it opened almost immediately. Ruth, in her skirt and tightly laced bodice, her pert breasts clearly evident above the white ruffle, stood there, her eyes immediately drawn to the bulge in the Taskmaster's lap.

'Oh, um, I'm s-so sorry, sir,' she spluttered awkwardly. 'Sorry, miss,' she added to Fazath, and then took a retrograde step to close the door and leave them alone.

'No, don't go,' the Taskmaster said smoothly, making no move to distract from the evidence of his excitement, induced by talk of the very girl who now stood peeping sheepishly at it from lowered eyes. 'Come in, my dear, and close the door behind you.' He smiled, and gave Fazath a surreptitious wink. 'You are Ruth, the innkeeper's daughter?' Without shame he cupped the bulge and gave it a suggestive squeeze.

'Really, I must go,' Ruth blustered. 'I should not have...' But she made no further move to retreat, only stared at the Taskmaster's impressive swelling, being rhythmically moulded through his hose by one hand. Then Ruth's brow furrowed endearingly as she pondered the situation. She looked from the Taskmaster to Fazath, and then back to the Taskmaster, her eyes drawn again to his moving hand and the lump beneath it, her tongue instinctively moistening her pouting lips. And still she made no move to close the door or leave the room.

The Taskmaster smiled and held out his free hand in invitation. 'Come here, my dear,' he said silkily, luring her to him. 'Come and sit with me.'

Ruth glanced shyly at Fazath, as if silently asking what she should do, and when the woman nodded she closed the door and moved, as though in a dream, unable to do anything else, to the sitting man. He smiled up at her, patted his thighs, and the girl perched elegantly upon them.

Fazath, resigned to the Taskmaster getting what he wanted and now hoping he'd take his pleasure quickly so they could leave the potentially dangerous place, watched anxiously as he stroked the upper slopes of the girl's breasts, pushed up by the tightly laced stomacher, and watched the beautiful innocent's head loll back as he leaned forward and kissed the milk-white flesh, burying his face in the soft warmth of her shadowy cleavage. Oh, how the woman envied him!

'A virgin,' he sighed between kisses on the upper slopes of her luscious twin globes, 'but a willing slave.'

He looked up at Fazath; whose eyes sparkled with envious excitement and real concern that the longer they stayed the longer they courted trouble. 'We once knew a girl just like you, my dear,' he whispered enigmatically. 'Did we not, Fazath?' He spanned Ruth's waist with a strong arm, so tightly nipped by the stomacher, and allowed his hand to slide down over the swell of her bottom.

Fazath sighed. 'We did. Poor Babala; perhaps we shall never see her again.'

Ruth's breasts lifted invitingly as she breathed deeply, trying to control her confused emotions. Her hands lay together in her lap, mere inches from the column of turgid flesh that lay coiled in the confines of his clothing. She lowered her eyes attractively and looked down at her feet, anxiously nibbling her lower lip.

The click of the door being locked sounded loud in the room and Ruth looked up, startled, and then turned to Fazath, and then to the Taskmaster.

'Do you know of the girl we talk about?' he asked.

Ruth shook her head. 'No sir, I don't think I do.'

'Are you sure, my dear?' he persisted. 'Do I need to put you over my lap to get to the truth?'

'S-sir?' she stammered, looking round to Fazath for support, and the Taskmaster used the advantage of her distraction to grasp her waist and flip her over his knees. She squealed instinctively, but Fazath, now understanding his insistence on meeting the girl, was quick to plug her mouth with a flannel she found beside the requisite bowl of water.

'I'm going to lift your skirt now, my dear,' he said, his voice betraying nothing of the excitement that Fazath knew he felt. 'And then we'll see how much you know about the girl we seek.'

'Mm, mmmm,' Ruth protested incoherently, kicking her dainty feet and struggling unconvincingly against the strong hand that pinned her wrists into the small of her back.

Fazath watched the spanking in silence, breathlessly turned on by the erotic scene; the girl twisting and writhing on the man's lap, him holding her there with relative ease, his free hand lifting and sweeping down to strike the delicious twin globes of the girl's quivering bottom with relentless precision. What a delicious sight!

The girl's eyes were wide with chagrin, and they glistened wetly as tears of shame meandered down her flushed cheeks, soaking into the flannel that shaped her lips into a perfect O. Her breasts, squashed against the outside of his thigh, heaved as she sobbed and their ripeness threatened to spill from the tight confines of her bodice with every juddering strike on her rear. How Fazath yearned to bury her face in that beckoning cleavage!

The mouth-watering buttocks quaked as the hard slaps rained down, and the girl mewled with pain and pleasure and her feet stilled as confusion and tiredness took their toll. The Taskmaster's hand slowed and the power behind the blows eased, and eventually stopped altogether, and the girl slumped wearily over his lap, her hair sweeping the floor.

With practised ease the powerful man lifted her once more into a sitting position on his lap, savouring her sweet grimace as her punished bottom came into contact with his thighs, enjoying her delicate weight pressing down on his immense erection.

As Fazath was drawn closer by the delicious site of the submissive girl sitting meek and exhausted, and placed a comforting arm around her shoulder, the Taskmaster kissed the salty tears that stained her pink cheeks.

'Now, what do you know of the girl we seek?' he asked again in gentle tones, lightly undoing the laces of her bodice as Fazath cuddled her and kissed the top of her head.

'Honestly, sir,' Ruth responded in hushed tones, seemingly unaware of the hand working at her front. 'I don't know who you are talking about or anything about her.'

The Taskmaster looked at Fazath, his hand finishing its task with the laces and slipping inside the tight bodice to mould one of the girl's firm breasts, her nipple hard against his palm. He nodded, almost imperceptibly, and Fazath gave a faint smile of agreement, understanding his meaning.

'Very well, young lady,' he said. 'If you say you know nothing, then we believe you. So we will go now and leave you to your evening duties.'

'Oh...' The girl frowned, disappointment furrowing her brow.

'Unless you would like us to stay a little longer...' he coaxed, reading her emotions with ease.

'I think I would, sir,' she said honestly, 'but I am a virgin and I must stay that way. My father would kill any man who took my innocence before wedlock.'

'We understand that,' said Fazath, kissing Ruth's hot forehead, the allure of the girl overriding her concerns of outstaying their welcome.

'But you do have a delightful bottom,' the Taskmaster hinted carefully, not wanting to alarm the girl. 'And it would remain our secret. Your innocence will remain intact, and your father will never be any the wiser.'

Ruth, fully understanding his meaning, blushed even deeper as she pondered his suggestion. 'But, it would hurt, surely?' she said.

'We will make sure that you feel nothing but pleasure,' he assured her.

'How?' she asked, unable to hide her desire to consent to their wishes.

'As the master penetrates your bottom I shall attend to your cunny,' Fazath told her. 'How does that sound?'

'It... it sounds heavenly, mistress,' she admitted, and her lips peeled open to accept the woman's passionate kiss as the Taskmaster fully opened her bodice and lowered his head to suck one of her rigid nipples into his mouth.

'Come then, my dear,' he said, releasing the delicious orb after a few minutes of very pleasurable suckling, 'the Lady Fazath will take you to the bed...'

Chapter 12

Babala, relieved of her chains, was left in the market square amid the garbage; the spoiled tomatoes, the rotting cabbage leaves and the trampled root vegetables.

She was hungry. Maxim's guards had been sparing with the scraps they'd fed her, and she was terribly thirsty.

She nibbled on a cabbage leaf and examined a carrot, which did not seem to be too spoiled. It was better than nothing, at least. Despite her awful predicament she could not help fearing for the welfare of dear Huru, and she wondered how he was, left by Maxim's men in the forest. Once her ordeal was over, one way or another, she would go back to find him and take him to the safety of Ellipsis. She owed him that much, at the very least.

The market was closed, the stalls empty and dark, filled with shadows, and she heaved a sigh of relief that she would not be seen in her nakedness. She huddled beneath a stall, her knees drawn up to her breasts and her bottom chilled on the damp cobblestones, nibbling on her meagre meal. The cabbage leaf did nothing to appease her hunger, so she was about to start upon the carrot when she was startled by a voice nearby.

'I'm sure I saw a girl,' someone said. 'It wasn't my imagination. She was naked, with long golden hair; a real beauty.'

'What would a girl be doing in this place at such a late hour?' demanded another. 'You've been drinking too much ale, Malesin.'

'That couple in the tavern; the nobles,' went on Malesin, ignoring the accusation that he had one tankard too many. 'Didn't they say they were looking for a girl?'

'No, the woman was just a whore,' the other snorted. 'Didn't you see how lascivious she was?'

'I tell you, I saw a girl,' insisted Malesin, getting back to the main point.

Babala tried to make herself small, huddling in the darkest corner beneath the stall, her hunger and the carrot forgotten, but at that moment her wrist was grabbed and she was hauled from the darkness. She gave a small scream and tried to pull away from her captor, but she was much weakened by what she had suffered over the last few days and the man was as strong as an ox.

'What did I tell you?' Malesin beamed triumphantly. 'I knew I saw a girl skulking at the edge of the town. This is the one, the girl the nobles were looking for. I'm sure of it.'

'She is beautiful,' agreed the other, reaching out to cup her grimy cheek in the silvery moonlight. Babala again tried to struggle, but the men were far too strong for her and she was drained from her treatment at the hands of Maxim's guards.

'And what were you going to do with this carrot, girl?' asked Malesin.

'I - I was hungry, sir,' she said wearily. 'I didn't think anyone would miss it, since it was thrown among the garbage.'

'Mm,' said the other, a salacious glint in his brooding eyes, 'I could dream up a few better uses for it...'

But Babala wasn't listening, although she instinctively inched away a little as the two men crowded even closer, their rough hands taking sneaky liberties with her body. The men had spoken of two nobles...

'Talito, my friend,' Malesin croaked, 'this little minx is turning me on.'

'Let's get her on the trestle,' Talito panted, 'on her back.'

As they manhandled Babala she stared at them with unseeing eyes. What if the nobles were who she prayed they might be? She scarcely dared to hope, but her hopes soared nonetheless. Could it truly be the Taskmaster and the Lady Fazath?

'Come on, my little beauty,' Talito grunted as he half-lifted half-shuffled her back to a market trestle. 'We're going to have some fun together.'

'Wait, please,' Babala said quietly, as though in a dream, 'the nobleman... what did he look like?'

Hands mauled her thighs and breasts as she was shunted up a little so that her bottom perched on the edge of the trestle. 'What does it matter?' Malesin snapped impatiently. 'We've more pressing needs than any he might have,' and Babala felt her hand being pulled down by the wrist to cup an urgent bulge within his tunic. 'Ah...' he sighed heavily and pressed her fingers tightly around his shaft, 'feel that, girl. Feel what's awaiting you.'

What if the Taskmaster had come to find her? Would she be punished severely by the palace nobles? Or would she be welcomed home? Babala's tummy turned excitedly at the thought. Home! The safety of the palace and the pampering she had always been afforded there. She frowned, thinking of the Lady Fazath, and hoped the Taskmaster had punished her severely for taking her from the palace and putting her through weeks of torment.

Just then Malesin drew back a little, a cunning glint in his eyes. 'You know, I'll bet my last shekel there's a reward for this young hussy,' he said thoughtfully. 'I'll bet I'm right and she is the girl the nobles are searching for.'

'A reward?' Talito was suddenly more interested in his companion's words than the delicious girl sitting submissively at his mercy. 'Do you think?'

'It could well be her...' Malesin pondered, trying to appear wise. He dragged Babala from the trestle and looked intently into her face in the chill of the creeping dawn. 'Could there be anyone, a noble, who might be looking for you?' he asked her.

So exhausted was she that she hung her head and shook it. 'I don't know, sir. Maybe, maybe someone seeks me, but I can't be sure.'

'Well, are they or aren't they?' Talito butted in, the prospect of financial gain making him impatient. 'We don't want to go trailing back through the town to the tavern unnecessarily, but we do want to find the nobles if it is you they're searching for.'

At last Babala nodded. 'I think they might be. But I don't know whether there is a reward for me,' she admitted. 'The people you mention may be looking to punish me rather than reward you.'

'Oh, I'm going home,' said Talito, impetuously losing all interest in the lure of a reward. 'It's late and I can't be bothered with a babbling peasant. I want nothing more than to crawl into my bed,' and he slunk away towards a meandering alleyway set between some mean dwellings at the edge of the market square.

'Well, I'm taking her,' Malesin called after him. 'A coffer of shekels would feed my hungry brood for many a long day.'

Talito waved dismissively over his shoulder without looking back at his friend, and disappeared around a corner.

So Babala stumbled along beside the man, part of her hoping that the strangers they'd spoken of were the Taskmaster and the Lady Fazath, and a smaller part of her hoping it was not.

Chapter 13

Dressed in fresh silk robes, her hair washed and shining and her face glowing with happiness, Babala sank back into the deep velvet cushions of the carriage the Taskmaster had hired to take them back to Ellipses. Her legs were spread and the silk pushed high about her thighs as the Lady Fazath knelt between them.

'Your little cunny looks as inviting as the day I took you from the palace,' the woman said, and stroked the plump lips, petting them and stroking the golden curls, fluffed and combed to add to the sweet perfection. 'All those wretched men have not spoiled you at all.' She parted the outer lips to reveal the erect nubbin within, startlingly pink against the darker flesh. Her lips closed about the little bud and Babala sighed happily, bearing up mischievously to push her nubbin deeper into Fazath's warm moist mouth. A tongue stroked the succulent flesh, teasing it with petting strokes until Babala began to shudder into a glorious orgasm.

The Taskmaster slipped a hand into the bodice of her gown, cupping a breast and lifting it so that the hardened nipple peeped over the upper frill of her gown. 'So different,' he murmured, 'so very different.' He sucked upon the nipple, and the only other sounds were Babala's contented breathing and the trundle of the carriage wheels over the rough road.

'Am I to be punished?' she asked, when he raised his head.

'Punished?' he asked, stroking her flushed cheek. He sat close beside her and she could see the hardened thickness of his cock within his tight hose. 'Why should you be punished?'

'No, my dear,' Fazath answered, holding up her manacled wrists. 'It is I who am to be punished for taking you from the Prince.' She twisted her body around to allow Babala to see her specially designed gown, cut at the back to allow the whip to fall upon her flesh without hindrance.

Babala shuddered. 'Well, what is to happen to me?'

'I am going to marry you,' said the Taskmaster.

Babala looked up at him, her eyes wide with disbelief and surprise. She was about to shake her head, to say that she was no longer good enough for him, when the horses were reined in.

'Out!' bellowed a rough voice from outside the carriage. 'All of you in there - get out!'

Babala's eyes widened with fear.

'Bandits,' growled the Taskmaster. 'There are many on the borders of Brentasi and Ellipsis.'

'Out, or do you want to be shot where you sit?'

The Taskmaster opened the carriage door and helped Babala down.

'And you!' the bandit roared.

'I am chained to the floor of the carriage,' said Fazath, and she rattled the chains that kept her secured inside.

'No matter,' said the bandit, the leader of the gang of three. 'This one will serve.' He pulled Babala close to his horse. 'What say you, Gelput?'

The rogue named Gelput, a heavyset brute, grunted and reached out to tear at Babala's bodice, then stared hungrily at her bared breasts and nodded. 'Aye, she'll do for me.'

'And you, Patman?'

Patman finished tying the poor elderly carriage driver to the spokes of one wheel and tore the gown further until Babala's pussy and the milk-white flesh of her bottom could be seen. 'That and the coins this gentleman has in his purse will suit very nicely, Manto,' he concurred, indicating the Taskmaster.

'Have my money!' the Taskmaster growled vehemently. 'You're welcome to it.' He unfastened the heavy purse at his belt and threw it to the rogue called Manto. 'But I warn each of you; leave the girl alone.'

Manto took the purse and hefted it in his hands, clearly pleased with the weight. 'Tie him up, Patman,' he ordered, apparently unconcerned about the Taskmaster's threat, 'while I take the girl to that clearing over there for some fun.'

'You'll hang for this,' the Taskmaster promised, as the other two men restrained him by also tying him to a wheel of the carriage. 'Each of you; you'll hang for this.'

Babala looked over her shoulder at him with pleading eyes, as she was half-dragged, half-carried to the clearing. The new gown was torn from her and she was flung face down over the mossy trunk of a fallen tree. Manto said nothing but his breathing, rasping and quick, told of his excitement. 'Please, don't hurt me,' she whispered.

'Hurt you?' he said. 'Nay, my need is such that it won't take me long to reach my pleasure.'

She felt fingers prising open her bottom cheeks and the slippery globe of a cock butting at her rose-hole. She held her breath, awaiting the inevitable, and then heard him grunt as her tight entrance yielded and he was able to sink his cock fully inside her, and she pampered his thick stem, hoping she could make him come all the quicker.

'Haven't you finished yet?' Babala groaned and looked up; it was Patman leering at them, with Gelput beside him.

'Let us join in,' demanded the latter. 'I want my cock between those lovely globes too.' He lifted his tunic and hefted the stained leather pouch that held his penis. Babala could see the outline of its large dimensions, and closed her eyes in dismay.

Manto grunted and pulled his cock from her bottom, holding the thick column of flesh in his hands as he anointed her buttocks with his seed, but before she could prepare herself Patman rolled her over onto her back. She tried to close her thighs but they were pushed apart once more.

'None of that, little miss,' he warned, sinking down between her legs. He, too, had his penis enclosed in a pouch, but he quickly released the thongs that held it about his waist. 'Now lift your knees,' he ordered, leering toothlessly down at her as she whimpered, her cunny stretching open around his thrusting cock.

'She's tight!' he panted, stabbing his hips at her. 'Tight as a virgin!' and then the odour of humid male flesh enveloped Babala as Gelput straddled her face, his heavy balls brushing her forehead as he positioned his penis at her lips.

'Open wide now,' he giggled, and as she meekly acquiesced his helmet stretched her lips apart and the gnarled column sank between them, filling her mouth and nudging to the back of her throat. He squeezed a hand under her neck and lifted a little to alter the angle of her head, giving him better access into her mouth, and then began to move slowly back and forth on his powerful haunches, gleefully fucking her there...

'Babala! Wake up!' She could not believe it; she opened her eyes and the Taskmaster was bending over her. Was she dreaming?

'It's all over,' he said, picking her up, cradling her in his muscular arms.

'But... what happened?' she murmured, and tears of relief meandered down her pale cheeks. The three rogues lay nearby, unmoving, and she saw the stains of blood on their tunics and on the ground, and turned her eyes away, feeling the nausea rise to her throat.

'It was the Lady Fazath,' he explained as he carried her away from the clearing. 'She had her knives and the fools hadn't bothered to search her. Chained though she was, she managed to reach out of the carriage and cut my ropes...'

'And you killed them,' Babala whispered.

'I did,' he replied, but said no more.

'And what will become of the Lady Fazath now?' she asked softly.

'Well,' he mused, 'despite her being the cause of all the trouble we've been through, I'll make sure she resumes her position in the palace and is not punished further. After all, if it had not been for her we would all have our throats slit by now.'

They reached the carriage and freed Fazath and the nervous driver, and then with Babala wrapped in furs and snuggled close beside the Taskmaster they continued on their journey. She smiled to herself and relaxed with the rhythmic movement of the carriage as they drew ever nearer the palace of Ellipsis. Home at last, she thought contentedly. Tiring of Verity's version of love in which she must be entirely submissive and willing to be humiliated at every opportunity, Gabrielle decides to end it all and jumps from the side of his luxury yacht, upon which she had been displayed like a trophy to Verity's clients.

Rescued by a beach bum off Key West, Gabrielle realises for certain that she hates Verity, but when he, Tom, and Robbie, the beach bum, play cards for her, who will win?

You may also enjoy...

SAMANTHA'S DIARY

A HOTWIFE'S FIRST EROTIC ADVENTURE

D. Z. MORGAN

Printed in Great Britain
by Amazon